PUFFIN BOOKS
Editor : Kaye Webb

SHANTA

Children grow up fast in some countries. They have to, when hunger is never far from the door and water-carrying and field work begin at an early age, as they do in India.

Shanta was twelve the year her whole life changed, the year her marriage was arranged and her father took the whole family (and their beautifully decorated cow) from their peaceful village to the maharajah's city for the festival of harvest.

The busy, bustling city was a frightening place, with its superficial prosperity concealing depths of poverty she had never dreamed of, where coolies risked their lives leaping onto moving trains to get work carrying the luggage, and hungry children scoured the streets for orange peel. And through the city, watching and waiting, there prowled a sinister yogi, or holy man, with a cold, chilling gaze, who seemed far too interested in her own family, especially her tiny brother Kitto.

All in all, despite the wonders she had seen in the city, Shanta was only too glad to return to her home and its safe monotony, but it was then that she left her childhood behind her for ever . . .

For readers of eleven and over.

Cover design by Doreen Roberts

Marie Thøger

SHANTA

Translated from the Danish
by Eileen Amos

PENGUIN BOOKS

Penguin Books Ltd, Harmondsworth, Middlesex, England
Penguin Books Australia Ltd, Ringwood, Victoria, Australia

—

First published in Denmark 1961
First published in Great Britain by University of London Press Ltd 1966
Published in Puffin Books 1972

—

Copyright © Marie Thøger, 1961
This translation copyright © University of London Press Ltd, 1966

—

Made and printed in Great Britain
by Hunt Barnard Printing Ltd, Aylesbury
Set in Intertype Plantin

THE village was a group of red clay huts between the jungle and the river. A road wound its way from the river bank, past the well, and up between the huts, and disappeared in the thicket on the ridge of the hill.

There were nearly always people on the road between the village and the river. That was the way you took to go to other villages or to the big city.

On the road to the jungle you met no one except the boys with the goats. While they minded the goats, they ran around in the thicket and killed snakes. They never went into the jungle itself for that belonged to the wild animals. Nobody wanted to meet the tiger, the leopard, the wild boar or the hyena at close quarters, to say nothing of the great herds of elephants which roamed in the bamboo forest far to the north.

It was an afternoon in the weeks before the rainy season. A brown girl was sitting in the dust on the jungle road and threading scarlet flowers on a straw. The air was warm and still, and an occasional soft breath of wind made the flowers fall in a shower on the ground and in the girl's lap. They fell from the flat, leafless top of the gulmohar tree, and she picked them up and threaded them on her straw. She made them into a garland.

Lazily she rose to her feet, and placed the garland round the neck of Kempi who stood munching nearby. The cow rubbed her nose affectionately against the girl's arm, and in return she scratched Kempi gently behind one ear.

At that moment the dogs down in the village began to bark.

At once the girl was alert. She had forgotten to notice the sun: it was low in the sky, much too low.

The first pair of oxen were already on the way home from the field; the man was walking behind them with the plough across his shoulders. Was it her father? With fluttering sari and legs red with dust, the girl ran down to the village. Not until she had reached the houses did she see that it was the leopard-hunter. Out of breath, she slackened speed and gave a little gasp of relief. If only her father would come home really late that evening.

She had gone out early in the afternoon to get firewood to cook the evening meal. She had searched for a long time in the thicket and along the aloe hedges, but others had been there before her. Then she looked under the great tree of life, and after that under the mango tree. There must surely be a withered branch somewhere or a handful of dry twigs which would burn under the rice-pot. But the girl found nothing.

She grew tired and sat down under the gulmohar. The red flowers showered down around her and of their own accord her fingers began to fashion a garland. She sat there day-dreaming and forgot the time.

Now she was dreaming again. That would never do. She had come to a standstill on the road outside the leopard-hunter's house. She must hurry home. The rice wasn't cooked and there wasn't even any firewood to put under the pot. Soon they would all be coming home. Father was tired in the evening, he wanted food. If the rice wasn't cooked he got angry, and as soon as Mother came home from the well they began to quarrel.

The girl hurried on again. She decided to take a couple of the cakes of dried cow-dung on the wall to get the pot boiling quickly. But that was dangerous; if Father found out, he would not take her to the harvest festival in the big city, and she had been looking forward to that since the last rainy season.

Then she thought of Granny. Of course Granny would help her. She would say that it was she who had taken the cakes. Granny was so old that nobody dared to scold her. Father was certainly a little afraid of her. She had lived so long, and the gods had tried her so often, that she had become very wise.

The girl hurried into the house. A few dry twigs lay beside the hearth. She pushed them into the embers and the fire flared up. Quickly she ran out again, took two cakes of dung from the wall and placed them over the flames. Then she poured water from the earthenware pitcher into the cooking-pot and flung in a few handfuls of rice. The rice-jar was almost empty.

When she had put the pot on the hearth, she suddenly became afraid that the fire might go out. She had to get down on her knees to blow between the stones. Smoke and ashes flew out into her face. She blew and blew, and at last the fire was what a fire under a rice-pot ought to be.

The girl went out to find Kempi. The cow had come home by herself today. Perhaps she knew that the girl had no time to look for her. The two of them understood each other. The girl often walked a long way to find a handful of greenstuff for the cow, and Kempi, muching patiently, always listened to the girl when she felt unhappy and all alone in the world. Now the cow went by herself up across the terrace and into the yard where she lay down quietly under the lean-to and waited to be milked.

Out in the village street the women were coming home from work, in small groups. They had been collecting stones from the fields all day long. It was hard work, but the earth must be cleared by the time the rains came.

The girl's mother and grandmother detached themselves from one of the groups and went into the house. With tired and rather stiff movements, they put down their flat bamboo baskets

7

beside the sleeping-mat. Her mother took water-pitchers and a rope to go to the well. It was high time. The water must be fetched before darkness fell and the spirits came out: the spirits were dangerous, especially to women.

Grandmother squatted on the floor beside the fire. She blew on the embers a little and bent over to look at something under the cooking-pot. The girl hardly dared to breathe. The old woman straightened herself slowly. She sat quite still and did not look at the girl as she said:

'Those cakes were to be sold in the town to get money for your dowry.'

The girl hung her head. After a little while she said:

'I walked and walked the whole afternoon without finding a single dry twig, and I got so tired. Then I was afraid that you would scold me if the rice wasn't cooked.'

Grandmother got up and looked at Kempi who lay chewing the cud with a red garland round her neck. She shook her head.

'Child,' was all she said. Then she took a cooking-vessel to milk the cow.

'We must make two new cakes early tomorrow morning. My son won't notice the empty places on the wall tonight,' she muttered to herself.

The girl heard what she said and longed to ask: 'But supposing Father does notice the empty places now, Granny? Supposing he does?' But she didn't ask.

Mother came in at the door with the two full pitchers. She poured the fresh water into the big earthenware jars behind the hearth. It was dark inside the house now with just a faint beam of light from the fire. Mother slid her hands along the rafters and groped for the leaf plates and the tin mugs which were to be used for the evening meal. She knew where everything was, and hurried to have it all ready by the time Father came home.

8

He could be expected at any moment now. She glanced at the hearth; nothing had been forgotten.

Smoke drifted from the fireplace along the floor and out into the square courtyard where it rose straight up into the air. Mother squatted down and looked with anxious eyes at the rice which was bubbling and steaming in the pot. What would her husband say if the food wasn't properly cooked? Grandmother and the girl squatted beside her. They were all waiting.

Then Father came in with the plough over his shoulder and the bullock walking behind him. Little brother Kitto followed at his heels. Kitto was not big enough yet to wear more than a shirt that reached half way down his fat little stomach. Father put the plough down just inside the door and led the bullock over to Kempi.

In silence he walked across the courtyard to the living quarters and sat down with his back against the rough clay wall. Now it was important not to keep him waiting. Even before he had tucked his legs up under him, a leaf plate lay in front of him. Mother was already piling it with steaming rice and the girl brought him a mug of sour milk.

Without a word he began to mix milk and rice together. The women drew back into the darkness and watched him with frightened eyes. Then he began to eat, putting the food into his mouth with quick, rough movements of his right hand. A little later he smacked his lips loudly. The women looked at each other and nodded: the worst was over now.

As soon as Father had finished, he got up, belched and went out into the courtyard where Mother stood ready with water to rinse his hands. Not until then did the girl feel easy in her mind. Father's hunger was satisfied. He had already turned away from the hearth to go out on to the terrace and talk with the neighbours. They came as soon as he unrolled the mat.

When the women and little brother Kitto had eaten, the rest of the food was placed in a covered jar. The rats must not be allowed to get at it. The fire was extinguished and the milk was put away. Then it was time to steal out to the terrace and hear what the men were talking about.

It was always about the same thing at that time: rain. The rain that did not come, although the earth was so dry and hard that it was cracking. The heat increased but the rain did not come. In a few days there would be no rice left in any house in the village. What then? Could they all live on ground-nuts until the harvest was in? The new rice had not been sown yet. Why were the gods angry? What had the village done?

Cigarettes glowed, vying with the fireflies that danced restlessly in the shadows along the village street. The men talked and talked in the warm darkness, but each was certain that he was not to blame for what was happening.

The girl knew many people in the village who might have caused the gods to be angry. Perhaps the drought had come because the headman beat his wife too often? Or because his neighbour let his children work harder than grown men? Or was it Father and Mother who were to be punished because they were always quarrelling so that evil words were spread about? It could also be that the gods had seen that the laundry man was much too hard on his donkeys. Or perhaps they were angry because nobody in the village gave any food to the dogs, but threw stones at them.

It was strange that the grown-ups didn't think of all this. The girl grew drowsy listening to their talk. Kitto was already asleep with his head in Mother's lap.

Granny stroked the girl's hair and whispered: 'Go in, I am coming.' 'What about the milk, Granny?' asked the girl. Granny nodded. She knew what the milk was for.

The girl slipped quietly into the darkness under the roof. She took a flat tin lid and poured in enough milk to cover the bottom of it. She placed the lid by the gutter in the wall. In the night the big black snake would come. He would look around a little, lick the lid clean, and go back by the way he had come.

The girl stole out again. She rubbed her cheek against Kempi's head and scratched her behind the ears. She did this every evening. The bullock was not forgotten either; he got a little pat on the neck before the girl lay down on the sleeping-mat.

Next morning the village was full of activity. The night before, the people had decided to make a sacrifice to the rain god. From every house folk brought a little of such foodstuffs as were still to be found: rice, ground-nuts and coconuts. But from the headman's house came earth mixed with the blood of a hen. The temple priest struck a bell while all this was offered to Gangamma, Gangamma who is in the rain, the river, the tank, the well, in every drop of water on the earth.

The girl was pleased when she saw them all going to the temple. As soon as the grown-ups were out of the house, she hurried to sweep up the dung that Kempi had let fall during the night. She mixed it with water in an old cooking-vessel, carried the vessel outside, took a big handful of the contents and slapped it down in one of the empty places on the red clay wall. But the cake was much too small. The others had the shape of Granny's hand. Hastily she took another handful from the cooking-vessel and slapped it on. She drew the outline of Granny's hand in the soft mass and stepped back to see if the cake was like the others. Yes, nobody would be able to see any difference. She made another one of exactly the same size and then went about her morning's work.

When the grown-ups came home, the house had been swept and the floor strewn with cow-dung and fine patterns of white chalk were scattered all over it.

'Shanta is a capable girl,' said Mother.

'It is time to think about a husband for her,' said Grandmother.

'Where shall we get the money from?' grumbled Father. 'She is dark-skinned, the bride-price will be high. Besides, we shall have to buy ornaments and saris and give food to the whole village.'

Mother and Grandmother said no more, for they knew nothing about money matters. After the harvest, Father hid his money in small jars that he put in the cavities in the clay wall. Nobody knew where they were for nobody saw him hide them. But everybody knew that he wanted to buy more land with the money. He wanted land by the river, for it was easy to water the rice there if the rain did not come.

I am the girl Shanta. Shanta means Spring. Mother gave me that name because I was born just after a rainy season.

What I am going to relate happened when I was twelve rainy seasons old. I was almost grown up, but all the same I didn't care to hear talk about marriage, and so I took little brother Kitto by the hand and went out of the house, away from Father, Mother and Granny, away from all grown-up people. We went over the rocks and down to the tank where the crocodile was killed. The tank is a long way from the river and there is no watercourse between them, so it is a puzzle to know how the crocodile came to be there. Could it have crawled from one flooded rice field to another, or was it a god who had made his home there in the water?

Two men from the village took it by surprise while it was basking on the rocks. They killed it with their hoes, then carried it away and laid it in front of the temple. Even though the tank was dry, there was still something unpleasant about the place, so I picked Kitto up and placed him astride my hip, and we hurried on.

It was the school we were going to. It lay a little apart as if it were too fine for the village, and indeed it was different from the rest of the houses. The walls were very strong and were white-washed from time to time. The roof was of red tiles, not the ordinary kind from the village, but tiles made in the town: they had been brought up the river by boat, and carried in bullock-carts the rest of the way.

While the school was being built, I went up there every day. It was finished just before the rainy season and for a whole day and night there was a festival in the village with drumming and dancing as if for a wedding. Fine folk came from the town and spoke to us about what a school is, but I didn't understand their long words.

Afterwards I asked Granny about it. Granny never went to school, but she is old and the gods have given her wisdom so that she knows everything. She said:

'In school you learn how to put thoughts down on paper and take the thoughts up from the paper again.'

She took the holy book down from the rafters and showed me the small black signs on its pages. 'These signs tell all the stories of Rama, Sita and Krishna,' she said as she carefully turned over one page after another.

I knew all these stories, for Granny had told them so often. From that night it became my greatest wish to go to school.

13

'But,' said Granny, 'going to school means that we must buy you a new sari; you cannot sit among the others like an outcast.'

I began to wish then that I could have a new sari. Before this, I had never thought about how my clothes looked.

One evening when Father was in a good humour, Mother asked him whether I should be sent to school. But Father grumbled:

'For a girl, a dowry is more important than schooling,' and that settled the matter.

I didn't go to school, but every day I took Kitto with me to the schoolhouse door. It always stood open, so I was able to follow everything that the teacher taught the other children. I liked the songs especially.

Everything was different that year. The gods kept the rain back for several weeks. The sun burned so that the earth cracked; there was not a drop of water in the tank and even the well was dry. Men and beasts became more and more tired and listless.

One afternoon when I was sitting with Kitto under the gulmohar and singing about the life-giving rain, a yogi came walking towards us. A yogi's coat is the colour of a ripe orange, and so I could see from a long way off that he was a yogi. He had a staff to lean on and a pouch in his hand. I wanted to run down to the village at once and tell them that he had come, for this was a great honour for us all; we should have to offer him gifts and listen to his words as he sat under the tree. But this yogi did not sit down. He said:

'Girl, I am thirsty. Give me water!'

There was no water in the village, so I only shook my head. The yogi's voice sounded so harsh that Kitto crept behind the tree. I too was afraid, for the yogi's eyes were cold. Perhaps he would put a curse on our village; Granny said that a yogi had power for both good and evil.

He looked out over the fields towards the dry river bed. Then he said: 'The gods are angry here. Why?'

I dared not move for perhaps he was Kali the evil one in person.

'Men are wicked. One day they will receive their punishment,' he concluded. Then he struck the ground hard with his staff, turned his back upon the valley, and strode angrily away. A yogi often says things of this kind, but I felt that his words boded ill to our village. Kitto was whimpering with fright as I set him on my hip and went home.

That night the rain came. Even before the sun went down it grew quite dark. Heavy purple clouds rose up like strange towers in the sky. More and more of them gathered and they grew darker and darker until at last they seemed to fill the whole space between earth and heaven. The air was stifling, but Granny said that she could smell water: Gangamma was near.

Then the first lightning flash tore through the clouds like a zigzag of fire. A clap of thunder followed. Kitto thought the sky was falling, and Kempi gave a long, mournful bellow. There were a few violent gusts of wind and a moment later the rain poured down upon the land.

The village street became a watercourse with a raging torrent that foamed down to the river. If a pair of sandals or a cooking-pot happened to be standing outside a house, it was carried away to the valley with the violent force of the current. The courtyard became a lake. The gutter could not take the water; it bubbled out at the door and down over the terrace.

Kempi and the bullock shifted from one foot to the other in water that came over their hooves. Only against the innermost wall of the house was it dry enough to spread the sleeping-mat. But nobody slept that night. Everyone in the village lay awake and listened to the varied sounds of the rain.

About sunrise the rain stopped. It was a glorious morning. The whole village looked new, the roofs, the palm-trees, the gulmohar and the tree of life. Everything was clean and newly washed. Water dripped from the trees, and a haze of heat and moisture hung over the valley.

In the village street the goats hopped from stone to stone, not wanting to get their legs wet. But when some dogs ran among them the goats panicked and most of them got wet right up to their knees.

As soon as the earth was thoroughly soaked the rice was sown, and soon afterwards it had to be transplanted. I was to go to the rice field for the first time. Granny had made three hats of banana leaves which covered the back from head to knees. When we went out early in the morning we bound up our saris and put on the hats. Women dressed in the same fashion came out of the other houses. The leopard-hunter stood on the terrace and laughed at us, and called us 'dung-beetles'.

First of all we went to plant in the landowner's field. He paid eight coins a day if we planted for him when the earth was covered with water. Everybody needed money, so we let our own small plots of land wait for the rice plants until later.

It wasn't raining when we came down to the field. The land-owner's people gave each of us a bundle of wet rice plants. The bundles were heavy, and all of the same size: I had to clutch mine with both hands. How was I going to manage the planting? Granny, who was just in front of me, turned round quickly and took a big handful of the plants. Now I could get on.

It had begun to rain again, a steady downpour. Granny placed herself at the head of the line and at once the whole row of stooping women started to move over the flooded field. The water reached my knees and the red mud on the bottom squelched between my toes.

Every time I bent down to press a plant into the ground, the water came up over my elbow. I had to be careful not to lose my balance for the bundle of rice was still heavy to carry.

At noon it rained heavily again. Granny began to sing. Her voice was drowned by others and the song of the rice rose up in the rain. All day long I planted with the other women and at sunset I received eight coins.

The days went by and became weeks, and the weeks went by. The rain stopped. Soon it was harvest time.

Now most of the men were busy building bamboo huts with roofs of palm leaves on tall poles along the boundaries of the field. While the ears of rice were growing heavy, care had to be taken that no thief should creep in and cut down the grain under cover of darkness. Night after night the men kept watch and were on the alert for any suspicious sound.

Those men who didn't build pole-huts contented themselves with lighting a fire for protection against the cold and the leopards and, of course, spirits.

During those nights there was a special kind of atmosphere in the village. The women gathered together in the houses and the darkness was wonderfully alive. Now and then you heard shouts from hut to hut in the field. This meant that one of the men had found something suspicious, or that someone had been unlucky in a game of dice and had lost his whole rice crop to his neighbour.

It happened too that singing would suddenly rise loudly from a watch fire. Then the women knew that the men had got drunk on palm wine and the next morning, perhaps, the crop would have been cut and ruined by strangers who had come while they slept. The women were always a little anxious about what went on in the field during the night. My father never drank, for he wanted to buy land beside the river.

At last, when the rice was quite ripe it was cut and brought to the threshing-floor which had been well stamped down and strewn with cow-dung. Here it was spread out, and the bullock and Kempi had to trample on it until the grain was separated from the straw. Kempi didn't like this much for she was used to doing just as she pleased, but it helped a little when I walked with her. To and fro we went for several hours until at length Father gave us permission to stop.

It was pleasant to be in the fields at threshing time. People were happy – happy because the hard toil of cultivating the land was over, happy because there was rice in the jars again, and there was no longer any need to eat those eternal ground-nuts. Shouts rang merrily from threshing-floor to threshing-floor.

When the straw had been pulled away we saw that our threshing-floor was covered deep in brown kernels. In spite of the fact that the rain had come late, the harvest was good.

Kempi stood munching grass beside the aloe hedge and when she unexpectedly let fall a large cow-pat, Father hurried to pick a handful of flowers and place them in a circle around it: Shakti, mother of the earth, must have her due. We all had the feeling that this was a good day. We made a game of tossing the kernels into the wind, and the chaff hung like smoke over the field.

The day when there is rice in the house again is a feast day in the village. All the gods are taken down to the river to be washed: Gangamma cleanses them. In the evening, to honour both them and her, they are adorned with flowers and placed in boats which are also flower-decked. When it gets dark, men with torches in their hands go down to the boats and sail the gods up and down the river for most of the night. They glide along like tiny glowing islands covered with jasmine, oleander, hibiscus and gulmohar.

I don't know why, but that year was different from others. Mother, Granny, little brother Kitto and I sat in the darkness on the bank with the other women and watched what was going on on the river. That was the same as last year. All round us the women sat and talked of how beautiful it was and of other years when it had been even more beautiful. I didn't think that anything could ever have been more beautiful. It was so beautiful that you wanted to cry.

Perhaps Granny could tell me why it was like this. I crept close to her and whispered:

'Granny, do you think that it is different this year too?'

'It is always different, Shanta, nothing is the same for two years together.'

'But quite different, Granny, so beautiful that it hurts inside, so beautiful that you want to cry?'

'Little Shanta, many many seasons ago there was another evening like this one that hurt inside. Cry if you want to: it is because you are getting a grown woman's eyes to see with.'

Now and again Granny would say things like that that nobody could understand. She put her arm around my shoulders and pulled my head down into her lap, just as Mother does to little brother Kitto when she wants to comfort him.

Perhaps I ought to tell Granny about all the things that had troubled me lately – that Father wouldn't send me to school, that they said I was to be married, that I had met the frightening yogi, and that Father and Mother were so often angry with each other. Granny stroked my hair softly, and now singing rose from the river. I forgot about the beautiful things in the world and the ugly ones too, and fell asleep with my head in Granny's lap.

The time of the harvest festival was drawing near. It had been decided long ago that we should all go to it.

Granny told me about the maharajah's palace which was many times bigger than the temple and full of lights that shone like stars; about the streets in the town where people milled to and fro; about the coffee-houses where the cakes were sweeter than sugar-cane; about the shops with saris of silk and gold thread.

Silk! Who could understand what silk was?

'Silk,' said Granny, 'is as soft as Kempi's nose, and as light as the chaff that flies in the wind. It shines like the river when the moonlight falls on the water, and it slips through your fingers when you try to gather it up in your hand.'

'And gold, Granny, what is gold, then?'

'Gold can steal a man's thoughts away. The gods have hidden it in the earth; it is red and yellow and shining. The man who finds a lump big enough to set his teeth in will never need to go hungry again even if the rains fail. But gold is dangerous too: it can turn a good man into a bad one and rob the gods of his soul.'

A sari of silk, and with gold thread in it! That would surely be all the riches of the earth and perhaps I should be able to see such a one.

We were terribly busy in the house and the field during the days immediately before our journey. First and foremost, the rice we had harvested had to be put in earthenware vessels and covered up so that the rats should not eat it while we were away.

The leopard-hunter who lived in the house next to ours had promised to look after our five hens and to keep the village boys and the monkeys away from our coconut-palm. That palm tree was my mother's pride. It stood at the corner of the house, not far from the door, and it was always given every drop of water that we had to spare. Every year its stem grew a little thicker, and every year it produced new leaves and nuts. This year the leaves were just the right size for mats, and both Mother and Granny were clever at weaving, perhaps the most skilful in the village.

'Your fingers are not big enough yet for that kind of work,' said Granny, 'but one day when you are older I will teach you how to do it.'

There had been many more nuts than usual on the tree this year, and after they had ripened, Father climbed up and picked them. Sometimes they were so big that it was difficult for him to carry them under his arm as he climbed down from the tree, and their shell was fresh and green and so shiny that you could almost see your face in it.

Sometimes Father would cut the top off a nut with his sickle and then we were all allowed to drink a little of the fresh milk, but some of it was always put aside for cooking.

'Coconut is food fit for a king,' said Granny; 'to own a coconut palm is wealth indeed,' and she took a nut and put it carefully away so that later on we might enjoy the firm white coconut which is inside the shell. But usually Father took the nuts down to the shop at once and got money for them, money for my dowry, and money to buy land by the river. There was one special plot he wanted which had four big coconut-palms on it. The landowner was willing to sell it but the price was very high, and perhaps he would sell it to somebody else before my father had enough money for it.

Every single evening they talked about money out on the terrace. What price would rice fetch? How much would the buyer offer when he came to the village? Nearly all the men owed the landowner money; if they didn't get enough for their rice they wouldn't be able to pay him and then perhaps he would take their land away from them.

Our rice harvest had been good and Father didn't owe anyone anything, but he grew more and more obsessed with the idea of owning that piece of land by the river. At length he was neither sleeping nor eating and not even Granny dared speak to him about the festival to which we had all been looking forward.

One morning when we woke up, he had gone. Nobody had seen him go. Towards evening he came home again, hot and dusty. Nobody dared to ask him where he had been or why he had gone away, and he himself said not a word about it but straight away climbed the coconut-palm and fetched down a large coconut. He cut its top off and drank most of the contents; the rest he gave to Kitto.

That evening out on the terrace he laughed and talked more than he had done the day before, and the next morning he said to Mother:

'Get everything ready so that we can start early tomorrow. We will visit your mother's house on the way to the festival.'

Whatever it was that had happened to him the day before, it had saved the festival for us and we set about the final preparations at once.

Granny ground some rice and made rice pancakes, two big

piles of them which she carefully wrapped in banana leaves. Different kinds of spiced food which were to be eaten with the pancakes were also packed in leaves. She put sour milk in one coconut shell and a little butter in another. Father climbed the palm tree and gathered two fresh coconuts which he gave to Granny.

'Perhaps we won't sell these,' she said, 'we shall see.'

Mother took a bag of rice with her. 'We must remember to take a cooking-pot too,' she said, 'so that we can cook our rice in the evening over a fire by the roadside.' She laid fresh rice-straw in the bottom of the cart, and we took our sleeping-mat with us as well.

Father came in with three bamboos which he bound to the cart so that they formed a framework over it. 'If the sun is too hot we can put the sleeping-mat on them,' he said.

At midday we all went down to the tank to wash ourselves and our clothes. Granny had taken some pieces of an old sari with her, and when we came to the water we took off our own saris, twisted one of the pieces of stuff round us, and waded out up to our knees. Granny showed me how to gather up my sari in my hand before pulling it through the water and rubbing it on a stone to get the dirt out of it. Mother washed little brother Kitto so thoroughly that he ran away from her and went and hid behind a bush.

While out clothes were drying on the rocks we had time to comb each other's hair and rub it with oil, and before the noon hour was over we were back in the village again.

Mother and Granny set about taking the cakes of dried cow-dung down from the wall and piling them into a flat bamboo basket. They were to be sold in the town.

I got permission to deck out Kempi who of course was coming with us. She was one of the family, and besides, it would be good for us to have her milk every day; perhaps we might sell some of it as well.

Kempi enjoyed having her whole body rubbed and brushed, and while I twisted strips of red, yellow and green tinfoil round her horns she lay quietly chewing the cud. It was only when I began to wash her hooves and paint them with gold paint that she really became interested and tried to lick the paint off: I had to hold her mouth and talk to her until it dried. I was determined that she should look beautiful. No doubt she was lonely at times because we weren't rich enough to have more than one cow, but at the festival at any rate she would be able to feel that she was the finest of them all. Luckily there was a little gold paint left over and I used this for the bullock's horns so that he shouldn't feel inferior to Kempi. All the hedges were full of flowers after the rains, so it was easy for me to weave a garland of flowers and mango leaves for both the animals. To keep the garlands fresh until the next morning, I put them in the water-trough in the courtyard.

That night I was too excited to sleep, and when the grown-ups were ready to go to bed I distinctly heard Granny say to Father:

'Perhaps it is time to buy a diamond for Shanta. She is too old to go about any longer with a splinter of wood in her nose.'

'Yes,' Mother ventured to say, 'I have heard that the people in my mother's village have grown rich since I left it. It would be a disgrace both for Shanta and for us if she were to visit my mother's house for the first time without ornaments and without a diamond in her nose.'

'Women have no sense,' grumbled Father. But Mother had started now, and she went on: 'Look at the leopard-hunter's daughters; they all wear a diamond in their nose although not one of them is as old as Shanta. Everyone in the village laughs at us because you are so mean.'

At this point Father became really angry and all his ill-humour of the previous day returned. But I knew that once Granny had got an idea he usually gave way in the end, so perhaps a diamond would be bought for me in the town after all.

Next morning we were all astir even before the sky in the east grew light. We washed our hands and faces, saw that our clothes were neat and tidy, smoothed our hair and wound it into a coil at the nape of the neck. Breakfast was quickly over; it was the rice left from yesterday's evening meal.

It was a fresh, chilly morning. Suddenly an idea came to me: I ran out and picked a handful of the white lemon-flowers that smelt so strong. Mother and Granny should wear them in their hair as the young girls do when there is a wedding in the village.

Mother looked at me oddly when I came in with the flowers. 'You are a good girl, Shanta,' she said. And I don't know why, but there were tears in Granny's eyes as she said: 'Put a flower in your own hair, my little girl: may the gods not make your life too hard.'

Father had already yoked the bullock to the cart and tied Kempi to the back of it. The flower-garlands made the animals look sturdy and well-nourished.

Granny took a last look round the house. Everything was neat and tidy. Just as she had shut the door and was about to put a piece of wood in the latch, I remembered the black snake; it wouldn't be able to get its milk every night but I could have given it some water. Suddenly I felt that all my pleasure in the festival would be spoiled if I didn't look after the snake. The grown-ups preferred to act as if they knew nothing about it, except Granny of course, and I myself wasn't sure whether I was afraid of it or fond of it. But Granny understood at once when I said: 'The snake, Granny.' She opened the door, and it took me only a moment to fill the lid with water and come out again. Then at last we were ready to start.

Mother and Granny took Kitto up into the cart with them. Father and I walked beside it along the village street. The high wheels creaked and jolted over the many stones in the road, and now Granny would fall against one side of the cart, now Mother would be almost lying on her back on the other. Kitto howled with fright and buried himself in the rice-straw in the bottom of the cart.

The scraping of the wheels and Father's cheerful 'ay-ah, ay-ah' to the bullock, woke the people in the houses we passed. The leopard-hunter, who slept on the terrace outside his house, sat up and said: 'May the gods look kindly on you.' On most of the terraces there were men who raised their heads and looked after us, and in many of the houses the women came to the door and waved to us.

When we had passed the last house in the village and had only the jungle and the river in front of us, I began to feel more and more strongly that there was something dangerous and much too unusual about this journey. It was odd that Father should have permitted it: he was always accustomed to refuse anything that wasn't strictly necessary. Was he really leaving home and wasting money just for the sake of the festival? Was there something about this journey that the grown-ups hadn't told me?

As so often before when something made me afraid, I sought comfort from Kempi. I felt so safe, walking with my hand on her warm neck. Kempi, however, was not at all pleased at being tied to the cart. The bullock was fresh and lively after a night's rest and stepped out briskly. Kempi wasn't used to moving so quickly. She tossed her head angrily so that all the glittering strips on her horns shone in the sun. Her skin grew dark with sweat and every time Father shouted 'ay-ah, ay-ah' to the bullock she snorted as if she had a fly in her nose.

It was not long before I grew tired with walking and running beside the cart, and when Granny noticed that my feet were beginning to get sore from the stones and thorns on the road, she took Kitto on her lap so that there was room for me to sit in the straw. At the same time, Father climbed up and sat astride one of the shafts and that made the load heavier. The bullock slackened his pace and Kempi jogged along after him more contentedly.

The whole of that morning we rode along by the river. We had to get to the other side of it. From time to time we saw a track that led down to a crossing, but the current was so strong and the water so muddy that we had no hope of keeping the cart on the flat stones on the river bed. If we missed them the wheels would stick fast in the mud.

Towards midday when the sun was high, we approached a village which looked exactly like our own. Father turned the bullock into the shade of a banyan tree by the river bank, and we clambered down from the cart. Then he unyoked the bullock and untied Kempi, and Kitto and I led the animals down to the river to drink. There was fresh green grass along the roadside, so there was no danger in letting them loose. They wouldn't run away.

When we came back, Mother had already given Father his meal. He had curled up with his loin-cloth over his head and was asleep close beside the trunk of the tree. Now it was our turn to eat. The rice pancakes had kept crisp and fresh in the banana leaf and tasted good with all the nice things Granny had in the other packages. All four of us were happy and gay and laughed a great deal as we ate until we could eat no more.

Mother told us about her mother's house where everything was finer than at home in our village, and no doubt the place had become richer still since she left it. Kitto tried to climb up to the aerial roots of the banyan tree, but grew frightened when all the monkeys in the branches came scampering down to see if he was one of them. He was terrified and started to yell. Father woke up and angrily told him to be quiet, and it was Granny, of course, who had to make peace again.

In the middle of the hubbub I suddenly noticed that Kempi and the bullock had gone right along the river bank to the village. A crowd of children had gathered round them and were admiring Kempi's beautiful horns. She was letting them scratch her behind the ears and looked very proud of herself, but when one of the strange children began to finger the strips of foil, I ran down and fetched both the animals and led them back into the shade.

When the sun was lower in the sky we drove on again, and towards evening we came at length to a place where there was a good crossing over the river. We saw a village not far away where women were going back from the well with their full water-jars, and men were taking the animals to the tank. Through the doorways we could see fires being lighted, and we could smell the smoke of the rice-pots. Everything was the same as at home in our own village, but we were strangers. Who would give us leave to light our fire and spread our sleeping-mat?

Father made for the tank at once. We women huddled together in the bottom of the cart and covered our faces, for at that hour there were mostly men at the tank who had come to wash themselves and water the animals. Father got out of the cart and went up to the men. He raised his hands respectfully in greeting, and then most of them came up to him and greeted him in return, gathering round him. He told them where we came from and where we were going to, and the men asked him about people they knew in the villages on the other side of the river.

They were all very friendly to us. We were allowed to cook our rice outside the temple and spread our sleeping-mat beneath the statues of the god.

When we left the village the next morning to drive out to the high road, we saw a yogi coming towards us. He was in a hurry, and as he strode along his coat swung around his legs. Perhaps he was going down to the river to bathe. As he went by without looking at us or turning his head, I recognized him: it was the yogi with the cold eyes. Was he an evil omen?

Towards evening we came to my mother's village, but she didn't recognize it at all. She hadn't visited her mother's house since little brother Kitto was born, and then the river had looked like our river at home. Now it was quite different. A dam had been built so that the water formed a lake above it, while below it poured down like a waterfall over a great flight of steps.

None of us much liked the idea of venturing on to the dam, but we had to do it as it was the only way over to the village. Luckily at that moment a tanga drawn by a horse came out from the village. I knew what a tanga was, and a horse too, for once the landowner had driven into our village in one. The tanga bowled rapidly on to the dam and Father tugged at the bullock's tail to make him follow it.

Kempi, stepping sideways on her gilded hooves, ran now to one side now to the other. She couldn't make out where the roaring of the water came from. At length she put her head into the cart so that I could scratch her nose all the time.

On the other side of the river we entered a grove of palm trees. It seemed to me like an enchanted land, with the swaying stems growing closely together, and the heavy crowns of foliage where the leaves brushed against each other with a dry, rustling sound. Was it betel, growing at the top of the stems?

'It is wealth to own a coconut-palm,' Granny was accustomed to say. Just think what wealth there was here in this one place!

'These folk are rich,' Father muttered to himself or to the bullock. 'Their wealth comes from the dam. Who can understand the gods? A temple used to stand where the lake is now.'

Now we rode down the village street. 'It is like a strange place,' said Mother. 'I can't even see my mother's house.'

'Didn't it stand opposite the well?' asked Granny. 'There's a big white house there.'

'Yes, but it's not that one,' answered Mother. 'Wouldn't I know the house where I was a child? It had walls of red clay, and village tiles on the roof, and we always put the cakes of cow-dung on the wall that faced the river.'

Cow-cakes on the wall of the big white house in front of us! No, such a thought would never enter anyone's head. But as this was Mother's village the house must be somewhere.

For once, Father had nothing to say about what we should do, and Granny was silent too. The bullock had stopped beside the well and Father just sat gazing over the fields to the west. The sky was cloudless and the sun was setting, red as a water melon. I don't think it was the sunset he was looking at; I am sure it was the fields that lay one beside the other, covered with water and with the haze of green that tells of newly sprung rice.

'Water on the fields in the dry season. Newly sprung rice a month after the harvest. And the water comes from the lake behind the dam. All of it the work of men. The temple used to stand there. Who can understand the gods?' said Father wonderingly.

Now the door of the big white house was opened from within. It was a heavy door of dark wood with gods and lotus flowers carved on its frame. A man came out on to the terrace, pulled the door to after him, and put his feet into a pair of leather sandals that stood on the top step. He was dressed in a long dhoti over which he wore a white shirt. He had a curious brown cap on his head and a long black umbrella in his hand. The sun's rays caught something on one of his arms and made it glitter and sparkle.

Father still sat without speaking or moving, and at the sight of this man Mother and Granny quite forgot to pull their saris over their faces, but I couldn't take my eyes off the thing that glittered and shone on his arm. Of course I had to ask Granny what it was.

'Granny, is that gold?'

'Hush!' said Granny, 'that is something that measures time.'

The man had certainly not seen us. He was leaning on his umbrella and looking far out over the fields, just as Father had done earlier. At last he began to go down the steps and so caught sight of us. He was surprised and came quickly towards us.

'Kamala!' he exclaimed. 'It really is my sister and her family! Come in!'

Mother looked a little shyly at him and said: 'My brother has changed. The village has changed. And where is my mother's house?'

The man smiled and his eyes were kind. 'The dam has changed the village and your mother's house has gone,' he said.

'But if my mother-in-law is dead, why didn't you send for us?' asked Father quickly.

'She is not dead, thanks be to the gods. She lives in my house. That house there,' he said, and pointed with his umbrella at the big white building behind him. 'But come in, come in. This house is your house also for as long as you wish to stay here,' he continued.

Father jumped down from the cart, lifted Kitto down and stood him in front of my uncle.

'We bring a son to my mother-in-law,' he said proudly, 'so that she can bless him before she dies.'

'The old woman will live many years yet,' said my uncle.

Now it was my turn to be pushed in front of him, and my mother said:

'This is Shanta whom you haven't seen since she was crawling about on the ground and playing with sticks and straws.'

'And now she looks to be ready for marriage,' he said kindly.

As he spoke, he turned to Granny who had been the last to clamber down from the cart. He raised his hands respectfully in greeting and bowed before her. Then he signed to us to follow him up the steps.

He opened the heavy door and went in first. We followed him into a big room that was in semi-darkness. The floor, of brown polished stone, felt smooth and cool under our bare feet. On the walls hung pictures of gods with wreaths of flowers and fresh mango leaves around them.

My uncle clapped his hands and a boy came running up with a mat which he quickly unrolled on the floor. With a wave of his hand my uncle invited Father to sit down. Then he went to a door at the far end of the room, pulled the curtain aside and called:

'Mother, Mother! Some people have come from a long way away to visit us.'

The light tread of bare feet was heard and an old woman came in. When she caught sight of my mother she held out both hands to her and drew her into the other room.

'Kamala,' she said, 'you have waited a long time to visit us, but thanks be to the gods that you have come.'

When my eyes had grown accustomed to the semi-darkness, I saw that there were several women in the room, and children too. Many people lived in my uncle's house, so many that during the time we were there I didn't discover who they all were and whether I was related to them all.

Without turning her head, my mother's mother gave the order that she wanted a mat, and at once a girl of my own age came with one and unrolled it behind her. She sat down, and invited first Granny and then Mother to sit beside her. Kitto kept close to Mother. She pushed him in front of the old woman, saying with pride in her voice:

'I have brought you a son, Mother.'

And I knew that she hoped the old woman would bless him.

'A son is wealth for a woman,' she said. 'The gods have been kind. May they long watch over him.'

Mother looked pleased.

'But Shanta, where is Shanta?' asked the old woman. 'She must have grown a big girl by now.'

I was finding everything so strange that I had kept in the background and was standing just inside the door: it is best, too, for a girl to be modest. It hadn't occurred to me that my mother's mother couldn't see very well any longer. I went and stood in front of the old woman.

'Come closer,' she said, 'and sit down.'

I sat down in front of her. She looked at me, and passed her hands over my neck and my body.

'She is indeed ready for marriage,' she said. 'A pretty girl, perhaps a little dark but we are like that in our family. She is one of us.'

'She is a good girl,' said Granny.

All the women and children in the room had seated themselves around us. Some were dark-skinned like the old woman, others were lighter like my mother. But all of them were better dressed than we were, and they watched us inquisitively, without a trace of shyness. My mother's mother kept looking at me.

'She still wears a splinter of wood in her nose,' she said in surprise. 'Why hasn't she any ornaments?'

My mother hung her head in embarrassment. Although Father and Mother often quarrelled, Mother never said anything disparaging about Father to anyone else.

'A marriageable girl must have ornaments,' repeated the old woman.

Perhaps she didn't know that our rice-jars were often empty and that Father was putting money aside to buy land by the river.

'We thought of buying ornaments in the town,' said Mother quickly. 'Of course Shanta will have a dowry and a fine wedding too. But I married into a poor village, Mother. Nobody there is rich. We have only one rice-crop a year, and our harvest depends on the rain.'

It surprised me a little that Mother dared to speak to her mother in this way when all the women were listening. But the old woman merely bowed her head and said:

'At that time we were poor here too.'

'Rich or poor matters very little,' said Granny. 'Kamala has been a good daughter-in-law and shared our toil, and Shanta is a good girl.'

Now they brought in fruit and sweetmeats the like of which I had never tasted, and water in brass cups. For some time there was lively chatter about all the changes that had come to the village because of the dam. Rice could be harvested three times a year, coconut-palms could grow anywhere, and there were many betel groves. Mangoes, bananas and oranges also flourished.

Gradually it had become quite dark in the room. The women around us had disappeared, and from the next room came the clatter of cooking-pots and the harsh sound of spice being ground between stones.

The old woman stood up and said:

'Now the men will have finished; you must go and take your bath.'

We were very dusty and dirty after the journey, but none of us particularly wanted to go to the tank in a strange village at that time of the day. We stood there rather uncertainly until Mother said:

'It's late, Mother, and already dark. Perhaps we should wait until tomorrow.'

'No, no,' said the old woman, 'everything has been got ready for you.'

She went to the door and put her finger on a dark knob. Suddenly a great light sprang from the ceiling. It was stronger than the sun at midday. For a moment we saw each other very clearly. Kitto shrieked in terror and I pulled my sari over my face.

'Don't be afraid,' said the old woman, 'this is the new light that we get from the dam. It won't hurt you. It just helps us to make the night shorter.'

As we stood there without moving, she said: 'In the beginning I was afraid of it too, and even now it hurts my eyes. I will take it away again.' There was a click, and we were in darkness blacker than I had ever known. Little by little our eyes grew used to it again, and we saw, or rather felt each other as we were accustomed to do.

'Come with me now,' said the old woman, and we followed her through unknown, dark rooms and passages out into the courtyard. A bright light streamed out from a doorway in the house on the other side of the courtyard. It shone upon a bamboo which was thicker and stronger than any I had seen.

Two women were going in and out of the house. One was carrying water on a yoke over her shoulders and the other was bringing fuel.

'Come,' said the old woman urgently, 'the bath is ready.'

We approached the bright light with great hesitation. When the old woman saw this, she went and put her finger on the knob so that the light disappeared. Inside the house a fire was smouldering under a big tub of water which had already been heated. In another tub there was cold water. There was soap too, and dippers and pitchers to rinse yourself with. On a bench lay three clean saris, and beside them fine oil for the hair. Everything was like a fairy tale.

When, clean and happy, we came back to the big house, the men had eaten and plates had been set on the table for us.

Now I know what a table is, but at that time I didn't. I didn't know either how to sit on a bench. The old woman sat down first. She tucked her legs up under her as if she were sitting on the floor and we did the same. But we didn't feel safe sitting so high and Kitto wouldn't eat anything. He happened to push one of the white earthenware plates and it fell from the table and broke. A brass jug of sour milk rolled after it. Neither Granny nor the old woman scolded him, but for the rest of the meal he stood behind Mother and held tightly to her sari.

The meal we had was much finer than a wedding feast at home in the village: rice with nuts, coconut, vegetables I didn't know the name of, freshly boiled milk with saffron, rice pancakes bigger than Granny's hand, and so many sweet things that I had eaten as much as I could before I had tasted them all. Mother, Granny and the old woman belched contentedly when the meal was over.

We hadn't seen Father and the men of the house the whole evening, nor did we see them when the old woman showed us our sleeping quarters.

From outside, the house looked as if there were two houses one on top of the other, and so, in a way, there were. The old woman took us to a flight of steps that was so high that it went right up to the ceiling, and when we climbed it we came to several other rooms and a terrace just below them; but up here the terrace was called a balcony.

In the daytime you could look from the balcony over the street and the houses, the temples and the wells of the village, and far out over the dam and the rice fields. Now it was night, and the stars felt a little nearer up here than down in the street. The air was fresher, and even the lightest breeze was cooling.

Mats were laid out for us, and the old woman gave each of us a sheet. Sleeping under a sheet was something I had never tried before. At home in our village we slept just as we went around in the daytime, in our saris; except, of course, when the rainy season was cold and then we had a couple of coarse rugs. But to sleep with sheets in the dry season, up here, where there was a wooden floor, was something I couldn't understand.

The old woman went down the dark stairs with light, sure steps, and for the first time since our arrival we were alone. Mother and Granny decided in whispers that we should sleep on the balcony, under the open sky. It was safer than being in the unknown darkness in that strange and wonderful house. At first, Kitto didn't want to come outside with us. The balcony was made of wood like the floor we stood on, and it creaked a little when we walked on it. This frightened him, but he didn't dare to stay alone inside in the dark either.

We lay close together with our sheets pulled right up over our heads, but all the same I couldn't get to sleep. All the sounds of the night were strange. Where were Kempi and the bullock now? I wondered if the animals got as good food as the human beings. Kempi was used to my coming to scratch her behind the ears before bedtime. Should I get up and slip downstairs and see if I could find her in the darkness? No, I dared not. I wondered if there was still some water in the black snake's lid.

There was a sound of voices just below us. It was Father and my uncle and a man I didn't know. No, I was wrong, I had heard that voice before. But where?

'Don't you work in the rice field yourself?' asked Father.

'No,' answered my uncle, 'I hire men to look after the field and the coconut palms and the animals.'

'That must cost a lot of money,' my father remarked.

'True enough,' said my uncle, 'but since the dam was built, my land gives three rice crops a year. My people gather many coconuts and mangoes and I grow more betel than the whole of your village produces. So you can see that I have to supervise everything and sell the produce in the town. I may buy a house there soon, and start a coffee house for our caste. It would please the village people and earn money for me.'

'The rich man is the friend of the gods,' said the stranger.

'Well spoken, yogi,' said my uncle, and there was the sound of a heavy coin being thrown down.

'But your sons,' asked Father, 'where do your sons work?'

'My sons go to school in the town. The eldest will be sixteen before the rainy season. I have decided that he shall study as long as he likes. But living in the town is expensive, so I must look for a girl from a rich family for him.'

'That will be easy for you who are rich yourself,' said the stranger.

'Perhaps,' said my uncle, 'but young men have their own ideas nowadays. He will only marry a girl who can read, and he wants to see her before the wedding. Where can I find a family who will agree to that?'

'You are clever and know more about life than your son does. You will be able to make him change his mind,' said the stranger.

My father said nothing.

There was a long silence. Cigarette smoke floated up to us through the cracks in the floor. Then, quite unexpectedly, the old woman's voice was heard: 'My son's eldest son shall marry one of our own family.'

There was no answer.

A moment later, light footsteps were heard going to the women's sleeping quarters.

I had more experiences than I can count in the course of the following day, but what I remember best was something I overheard when we women had gone up to the balcony to sleep. Just as on the previous evening, the men sat on the terrace beneath, smoking, or talking together from time to time.

'The old woman thinks that your daughter will be a suitable wife for my eldest son,' said my uncle slowly.

My father must have been very surprised, for he was silent for a long time. At length he said:

'I am not poor. I have land for rice and land by the river with four coconut-palms. I can also give my daughter ornaments and saris and a dowry, but I am not rich enough to have a son-in-law who is studying in the city.'

Land by the river with four coconut-palms? I became wide awake. Where had the money for that come from? And the old woman wanted me as a daughter-in-law! None of us had thought of that. To marry someone who was studying; to go away from the village and the work in the rice field, from Granny and Kempi and the black snake; to live, perhaps, in this big house and have beautiful saris and many ornaments! Was I glad or sorry? In any case I felt uneasy about all the unfamiliar things in the world of the grown-ups.

My uncle spoke again: 'My mother, the old woman, who has seen all the great changes happen here, says that this marriage must be the will of the gods. She says: "How will it help us if your son is cleverer than the judge in the city if he forgets us and the land he came from?" She says, "Kamala's daughter is one of our own people. She will bind his thoughts to the family." We ought to give heed to the wisdom of the old folk!'

'Of course I shall be glad for my daughter to marry into your house,' answered my father. 'Nobody could train her better than the old woman here. And you will be satisfied with her dowry.'

'We must find out what the position of the stars was when the children were born. If the result is favourable, the wedding can take place in the next marriage-month as far as I am concerned,' said my uncle.

'Yes, I must consult the women to see whether Shanta is old enough,' said Father reflectively, 'but if they think the time has come, then I have no objections.'

40

'Perhaps you ought to see your son-in-law before we come to a final decision,' said my uncle. 'The school has closed for a week because of the festivities in the town, and all three boys are coming home tomorrow. If you delay your departure until tomorrow evening you can see him.'

'I had thought myself that it would be better to travel by night,' said Father. 'All the roads are crowded with people on the way to the festival. It's easier to get on at night.'

For the first time that evening, the stranger took part in the conversation. I knew now that he was the man whom in my own mind I was accustomed to call the yogi with the cold eyes. He offered his help in casting the horoscope. The men seemed to welcome his offer, but as before, I was afraid that the yogi would bring misfortune.

Mother and Granny had listened to the conversation as attentively as I had, but we didn't say anything to each other, not even after the men had gone. It was a long time before I fell asleep, and perhaps Mother and Granny lay awake longer still.

Towards noon the next day the three boys came home from the town. They were wearing dhotis and shirts like their father and they had put up their black umbrellas to keep off the sun. They carried their sandals in their hands. They were hot and sweating and their legs were covered in red dust.

When I caught sight of them, I hid behind the well. I don't think they saw me. The tallest resembled his father most. He looked at his brothers with the same kindly smile that I had already seen in his father. At the top of the steps outside the heavy door, he turned and looked out over the fields. At that moment I very much wanted to stand up, but luckily I did not, for it would have been most unbecoming.

Then and there, my fears about moving to the big strange

house disappeared. From now on I hoped that the position of the stars would be favourable for my marriage with my uncle's eldest son.

The maharajah's town lies in the centre of Southern India high up on the plateau. The land is flat and stretches as far as the eye can see. Here and there a rock rises steeply from the level plain.

Some gigantic god must have played here with stones from the mountains in the North. Or perhaps the god became angry with the people of the plain, and in his wrath hurled some of the mighty blocks of the Himalayas against them. The blocks fell upon the plain as mountains. They are still there, and in the shelter of the biggest of them the maharajah's town has grown.

Why just here? Who can say for certain? Perhaps it has something to do with Shiva's bull, Nandy the bull, as the people call him. He was made by men: hewn from the rock, he lies high up above the town.

He has not much in common with the scraggy bullocks of India. He is many times bigger than any of them and his limbs are rounded and full of strength. He has lazily drawn his hind legs up under him and laid his mighty body to rest on the mountain side. Only one foreleg, which is bent slightly forward, shows that he is ready when Shiva, his lord and master, calls.

His massive neck is adorned with many rows of balls and chains of intricate patterns. They are carved from the stone like himself. A stone bell rests on the powerful chest. He has no horns, but the flaring nostrils which are so big that a man can put his head in them, show that he is always on the alert. Perhaps he will rise up one day to carry Shiva over the plain with lightning speed.

The people at the foot of the mountain think that this is his destiny; therefore they honour him and make sacrifices to him. When he was young he was no doubt as grey as granite, but the many offerings of oil and other fats that have been poured over him in the course of the years have made him black and shining as marble.

He has been lying there for many hundreds of years and he will remain there until the mountain moves. With his eyes of stone he will gaze on the plain and its people. He will look down on the maharajah in his palace, on the beggar who has no roof over his head, and on everyone who lives in the town at the foot of the mountain.

The custom of celebrating after the harvest in the presence of the maharajah is an old one, but who knows whether the bull is not older still? Perhaps he has seen people stream in to that festival from the very beginning of all things, has seen them come year after year, thousands of dark figures in white dhotis and red, green and blue saris.

Perhaps this indescribably motley stream has changed a little through the years. But the ragged beggar who crawls along the road with his incessant cry: 'Baksheesh, sahib, baksheesh, sahib,' has always been there. So has the poor peasant who works in the rice field, and who has come year after year, often from a long way off, bringing his family in a cart. And the yogi in his orange coat with a necklace of walnut shells around his neck has never failed to be there either.

On the other hand, the wealthy factory owner in the bright-coloured, highly-polished motor-car is new, so new that he is noticed in the crowd. They make way for him as he pushes forward with his car load of silk-clad women, each of whom wears a small fortune in ornaments on her smooth shining head.

The modern farmer wearing khaki clothing and driving a jeep is new too, but somehow he fits into the picture.

Then there is the bus – the bus that rattles and clatters along the highways of India, with so many people outside and in that it is a wonder that someone doesn't fall off more often. That is new, but so typically Indian that it seems timeless.

Year after year, with unruffled calm, the bull has watched this living stream. He has seen it flow along the red roads to the town at the foot of the mountain. This year too, the year when the girl Shanta is to come to the festival for the first time, the bull takes part in it from the beginning.

He sees the town put on its holiday garb.

He sees markets spring up, and bazaars full of all kinds of cheap goods side by side with costly articles and displays of the country's best products. The town's own shops are swallowed up in the mass.

He sees snake-charmers with sleek, shining cobras which sway gracefully to the sound of the flute. He sees devil-dancers whose bodies are painted with bright colours and fantastic designs, and leopard-men with gorgeous skins on their backs, and the animal's terrible claws stretched out in front of them in a savage dance.

But first and foremost he sees that the town is filling up with people, more and more of them every day. At night they sleep on the river bank, in the temples, at the railway station, beside the houses, on the pavements and in the great square in front of the maharajah's palace. They huddle together, family by family, on the bare ground. When morning comes, they shake off the cold of the night and cook food over charcoal stoves and fires of dried cow-dung.

We came to the town early in the morning of the first day of the festival. Father let the bullock amble along as he pleased. We just sat and let all the new sights glide by us. Buildings, bigger than my uncle's house: shops, most of them with their shutters still up: people, sleeping, eating and trading. Everywhere, people we didn't know, strange people.

In our village you could walk in safety wherever you liked as long as the sun was in the sky. You could talk to the people you met and call them by their name. Perhaps the people here didn't even speak the same language as we did; they hurried to and fro in such a curious way and seemed to be terribly busy. They spoke loudly and quickly and threw their arms about much more than the people in our village.

We had now entered a street which was very narrow. Everybody seemed to be going towards some definite goal. Just behind us there was one of those peculiar vehicles that Granny called a car. It went along without any bullocks in front of it, and inside its nose was something that hummed the whole time. If we went slowly, the noise grew fainter, and if we increased our speed it rose so that it sounded like the growling of a wild animal behind us. Kempi hopped and danced as if a tiger were after her.

The street was so narrow that the vehicle couldn't pass us. The man in the car abused us violently and called us country bumpkins who ought to have stayed at home in our muddy rice fields. But it was quite impossible for us to advance more quickly before we reached the end of the street. Here there was an open square in front of a big building. High up on the white wall were some curious black figures and in the middle of them what looked like a pair of arms. One of them moved slightly from time to time. When I asked Granny what it was, she answered:

'That is a thing that measures time, like the one your uncle had on his arm.'

It was odd to think of measuring time in that way. Wasn't it enough to know from the sun whether it was time to get up, time to rest in the shade or time to go home from the field?

'People here don't live by the sun,' explained Granny, 'they can't always see the sun because there are so many houses. They live by that object that measures time. They call it a clock. Often they become confused about day and night because they have other light than the sun's. Then they look at the clock and say "What is the time?" '

Father had driven across the open square to the big white building, but there were so many carts and cars ahead that we couldn't find room. Not far off we saw a pleasant green field with many trees and lovely flowers.

'That's a park over there,' said Granny.

Father turned the cart, and we drove along beside a high wall down to the park. A pipe stuck out in the middle of the wall. Water trickled from it the whole time and people stood around it washing themselves. The men took off their shirts and dhotis, washed them and hung them up on the wall to dry. Then they stood in their short striped pants and washed their whole body.

The women washed their arms and their feet and rinsed out their mouths, but most of them were not bold enough to remove their saris completely from their faces while they did it.

The sound of a flute came from the other side of the building. Many hurried away, but those who had clothes to dry remained behind. They found a place where the wall cast a shadow and lay down to sleep, or perhaps they remained awake to see that no one stole their clothing.

Father tied the bullock to a large aloe that grew in the hedge in front of the park, and we climbed down from the cart. Before anyone had time to think what he was doing, Kitto darted off and stood right under the water. It came out just at the height of his head and he shrieked with fright when it ran down over his face and neck. In a moment his shirt was soaked. Mother took it off, washed it out and hung it over the side of the cart.

Father had gone towards a wide door in the middle of the big white building. Holding their saris over their faces, Mother and Granny followed him, and Kitto, without any clothes on, walked between them. I kept behind them. Father didn't go into the building. He stood beside the door and looked in, and from time to time glanced back at the cart and the animals.

Inside there was just one large room which was quite full of people; there were more, perhaps, then in the whole of our village. Most of them sat on the floor with boxes and bundles around them, staring blankly in front of them. Others had unrolled their sleeping-mats and were sleeping soundly with their belongings under their heads.

From the door came the scent of jasmine and lemon-blossom, stronger than the scent from the trees behind the leopard-hunter's house when they were in full flower. It came from piles of white flower-garlands which lay in flat bamboo baskets on the floor among the people and their bundles. Beside each basket sat a woman. These women were no better dressed than we were. They were all small and thin and very dark-skinned. It was early in the day, and most of them had so many garlands that they were completely hidden by the white piles in their baskets. There were more flowers than when the gods at home are washed in the river.

Before I was able to ask Granny about all the things that had come into my head, she said: 'Do you see the flower-garlands, Shanta?'

At that moment a prosperous-looking family passed us and went in through the door. It was a large family. There were many fat, sleek people, expensively dressed, with a number of coolies who were carrying boxes and bundles on their heads. The fattest of the men went up to a flower basket and began to rummage among the white garlands. He took the finest and gave each of his women-folk one to wear round her neck. They all laughed and talked a lot, especially when one of the men got a garland too. The children were given small ones. Then the fat man threw a coin into the lap of the woman behind the flowers, and they talked loudly and were very gay as they walked across the room and out of a door on the other side.

'People who are going on the train are given flowers,' said Granny.

But Kitto and I didn't know what the train was, so Granny had to explain: 'It is a great number of carriages one after another. They run on long iron bars which are called rails and which stretch from here to every town in the land. The carriages are pulled by a machine which puffs and hisses and lets out smoke and steam from time to time.'

'Why are people given flowers when they are going to travel on the train?' I asked Granny. 'I suppose it's to wish them a good journey,' answered Granny. 'Why did you pick flowers for your mother and me on the morning we left the village?'

I didn't give an answer to that for Granny didn't seem to expect one. But when I think about it, it was because I was happy myself and wanted to make them happy too. Just fancy, if I had had some money now I could have bought flower-garlands for Mother and Granny and Kitto and Father, and then all these folk around us would have looked at us and thought that we were rich people who were going on the train. Kempi and the bullock needed fresh garlands too, The flowers they had got at home in the village had long since become brown and ugly.

Father turned and went back to the cart. We followed him at three paces' distance, as is fitting when one is among strangers.

'We must find a place in the shade before the sun gets too hot,' said Father as he untied the bullock.

I was surprised that we couldn't just go into the park behind the hedge. The grass was beautifully green there, and the big trees gave shade. But Granny said:

'That will never do. They will be very angry with us if we drive in there with the cart and the animals.'

'Perhaps we could walk a little way along one of the small paths through the grass,' said Mother.

'Kamala is right,' said Granny. 'Shanta must get to know what a town is like if she is going to marry a man who is studying.'

Father just muttered, as he was accustomed to do when he meant to say that women have no sense. He sat on the shaft of the cart so that everybody could see that he was waiting.

Mother felt Kitto's shirt, but it wasn't dry. Granny said:

'What does it matter? Let him go naked. There are many boys of his age here who are not wearing clothes.'

Kempi shifted from one foot to another with boredom, and switched her tail at the flies. But fine as she was with her gilded hooves and glittering horns, she couldn't come with us.

Carefully and very respectfully, we others slipped through the gate into the park. We kept to the middle of the path, for Granny said we mustn't walk on the flowers or the grass here. The path ended in an open space. In the centre of it was a bed of unknown plants and flowers of beautiful colours. They smelt so strong and so strange that they made you feel dizzy. In the middle of the flowers a jet of water sprang up out of the ground and spread in a shower over the bed; the earth was muddy like a rice field after rain.

We went farther and came to a tiny lake, the surface of which was completely covered with lotus flowers. We couldn't go right up to it because grass had been sown around it. Instead, we walked round the grass, and on the other side, under a great bamboo, we saw two women.

'Look,' said Granny softly, 'their saris are made of silk.'

'And look, there is gold in the border,' whispered Mother.

'They have gold round their necks too,' said Granny.

To make room for them on the path we huddled together as close to the grass as we dared. We turned our backs to them and pulled our saris forward across our faces.

The women walked past us as if they didn't see us. Their saris swung freely behind them and both of them had their face and head completely uncovered.

'Just see what's coming,' said one of them suddenly.

'A cow,' laughed the other, 'a cow decked out as if it were the maharajah's own sacred cow adorned in all its glory for the festival.'

'How can you find that amusing?' said the first woman angrily. 'I think it's dreadful that these cows should be running about all over the place. You can't find peace even in the park, and the keeper just turns his back to spare himself the trouble of driving it out.'

'Don't be cross,' said the other one, 'just look at that cow. It's not an ordinary cow. I think it must have travelled for days on end to be at the festival. Why shouldn't it be allowed to take a stroll in the park?'

'You're joking about something serious,' said the first woman hotly. 'As long as we Indians have sacred cows, every other nation in the world will make fun of us. At home in England . . .' She couldn't say any more because the other one laughed so loud and long.

'The maharajah and the farmers and many other people worships cows, and you worship England. What is the difference?' she said, when she had stopped laughing. Then she stooped down and picked a handful of grass which she held out to Kempi. For it was Kempi who stood there in all her finery. The sight of her made me forget to hide my face. She had a wild look in her eyes. I am sure she knew that she had no right to be there and that she must get away at once.

The moment that the tuft of grass touched her nose, she sprang suddenly and violently to one side, and landed in the flower bed. Her gilded hooves sank deep in the mud. Terrified, she tried to get out, but fell on her knees a little farther forward. Her muzzle went down in the mud and her horns among the plants. Nervously she tossed her head back, spattering the fine ladies' faces with earth and flowers. Then she sprang on to the path, and rushed in a mad gallop with her tail in the air out of the open gate.

One of the women laughed until the tears ran down her face, the other shouted abuse at us. I didn't understand much of what she said, nor had I understood what their previous conversation meant, but I was terribly sorry that Kempi had destroyed all those beautiful flowers. Perhaps the keeper would come now and take her away from us. I was so afraid, that without giving a thought to the others I ran off to find her. As I went through the gate I saw that Father had fallen asleep in the cart. Kempi must have broken loose while he slept.

Now I saw her far down the narrow street. She was trying to

push her way against the stream of people and vehicles, but it was difficult and she was being driven back the whole time. When I reached her and began to stroke her neck and nose, she calmed down a little and willingly followed me back to the cart.

Father was very displeased with the whole affair. Nobody said anything about it, but we all knew that it had happened because he had gone to sleep. There was no sign of the keeper, and Father decided to move on somewhere else.

A red track full of pot-holes led behind the big building. We followed it in order to get away from the crowds and all the cars. The road ended under three palm trees beside the thing the grown-ups called the railway.

'This is a good place to stop,' said Granny. 'There is shade here, and we have water on the other side of the building.'

Father carefully tied Kempi to one of the palm trees, but he let the bullock loose. Mother put Kitto's shirt on and took him over to the railway.

'Look, my son, the trains run along those rails,' she explained. 'They run very fast and they are terribly dangerous. You must never go near them by yourself. They sound like thunder before the rainy season when they are coming. If you hear that, you must run back to us at once.' It was easy to see that Kitto was only half listening to what she said. He had invented a lovely game, putting heaps of small stones on the shining rails.

Now Granny joined in. 'Kitto, there is something else that you must remember,' she said. 'Never run so far away that you can't see us, and never go with anybody you don't know.' Kitto nodded eagerly, and went on playing with the stones.

'Come back now,' said Father, 'a train is coming.'

There was nothing to be heard and nothing to be seen. How could Father know that a train was coming?

'What makes you say that?' asked Granny.

'Look at all the coolies on the platform,' said Father, pointing to the big white building. 'See how they are sitting ready on the cement and beside the rails.'

They reached almost to the spot where we were, a long row of thin, brown men squatting beside the railway. They were a motley crowd; some were in blue working shirts and pyjama trousers, others wore only a loin-cloth, but all of them had enormous scarlet turbans on their heads. A few were smoking, others were chatting lazily together.

More and more people were gathering on the cement with parcels and bundles. We could hear the hum of their conversation.

'Listen!' said Granny, 'the train!'

Yes, it was the train, like distant thunder. At that sound, something happened in the row of coolies. Some got up and ran a few steps in our direction, others crept even closer to the rails. All were on the watch, like animals ready to spring.

The noise like thunder came nearer. There was the train! It looked like a black snake with smoke above its head.

One by one the men half rose to their feet. The red turbaned heads bent forward, and every muscle in their bodies was tense.

'In a moment they will spring,' said Granny. 'Poor wretches! They fight for food almost like wild beasts.'

When the train was level with us, it began to slacken speed. The coolie nearest to us stood on tiptoe to see which passengers had most bundles and boxes with them. He let two coaches go by, then, when the third came, he leapt forward. The train was still moving. He caught hold of a door handle and clung to it; then he got his feet on to a step. But now another man leapt for the same door and tried to push the first one down. They both fell, and a third man got hold of the door.

A moment later it looked as if a pitched battle were in progress. It was not a pleasant sight. 'Poor wretches,' said Granny again, 'food is hard to come by in a town.'

The train stopped. At every single window and door there was a jostling crowd of men in red turbans. When one of the passengers had chosen a coolie, the man piled boxes and bundles on his head like a tower.

'As high as three water-jars one on top of the other and as heavy as a bullock,' said Granny.

'But perhaps he gets as much for carrying that load through the town as a coolie earns for a whole day's work in the rice field,' said Father.

'Perhaps,' said Granny, 'but perhaps he isn't lucky enough to earn any more for many days afterwards.'

'Perhaps and perhaps,' muttered Father.

'His life is short,' said Granny, 'shorter than the peasant's. His children are left fatherless before they are able to get food for themselves.'

What a strange place a town was, at once much richer and yet so much poorer than our village.

By now the big white building was completely deserted. We made for the shade of the palm trees to have something to eat.

Two children came walking along beside the railway lines, carrying the bottom of a frayed bamboo basket between them. They were a boy, bigger than Kitto, and a girl who was a little smaller. Now and then the boy stooped down and picked up a banana skin or some orange peel, rubbish that had been thrown out of the train.

In our village I had never seen anybody pick up anything that someone else had thrown away. Why were they doing this? What were they going to use it for? It had been lying in the dust and trodden on.

Keeping at a polite distance, they passed us and sat down on the extreme edge of the shade cast by the farthest palm tree. They sat quite still and silent and watched us eating. Our meal consisted of the last of Granny's rice pancakes. When they were finished we should have to content ourselves with plain rice and Kempi's milk until we got back to our village. But we should have plenty, for the old woman in my uncle's house had given us a whole bag of rice when we left.

It looked as if Granny wasn't really enjoying her pancake. Could she be ill? The two children were still sitting there. Without taking his eyes off us, the boy stretched his hand out and found the skin of an orange in the basket. He divided it carefully in two, and gave half to the little girl. Still keeping their eyes on us, they began to eat the dirty peel. I felt a lump in my throat, and my hunger disappeared.

'Granny, look, they're eating what other people have touched and trodden on,' I said.

'They are hungry, Shanta,' answered Granny, quietly.

'Poor little things,' said Mother.

'If I gave them my pancake, would they eat it even though they don't know me?' I asked.

'They would, my child. Take mine too,' answered Granny, 'I am not hungry.'

'I don't want mine either,' said Mother.

'Yes you do, Kamala,' Granny hastened to say. 'You need all your food so that your new child may live.'

That was the first time I had heard that my mother was expecting another child. Of course it was great news, but for the moment I was more concerned with the two little strangers. When I stood in front of the boy and offered him the two pancakes, he got up. But immediately afterwards he threw himself flat on the ground in front of me, and touched my foot several times with his forehead. What did this mean? A feeling of misery overwhelmed me, and tears ran down my cheeks.

'He thinks the gods have sent you,' said Granny.

He got quickly to his feet and took the pancakes carefully. Without saying a word, he broke off a tiny little piece from one of them and tasted it. Then he gave the pancakes to his little sister. For a long time they sat holding their pancakes without moving.

'He knows that he can eat it,' said Granny, 'but perhaps they are too shy to eat proper food while we are looking on. Turn your backs. It would be a pity if they went somewhere else and people took the food away from them.'

We all turned our backs to them.

'Just imagine being so hungry that you eat refuse and take food from a stranger's hand,' said Mother.

In our village, one would only take food from one's family or those who belonged to the same caste. That was the custom.

'Custom doesn't really matter when it's a case of real hunger,' said Granny. 'Perhaps those two have to fend for themselves in the big city. There is no one to provide them with food or to teach them custom and usage, but all the same I don't think they are ordinary beggars.'

'No,' said Mother. 'It's odd that they don't say anything.'

There were no beggars in our village, but I knew that beggars were people who obtained money by looking pitiful and asking people to give them something.

'Perhaps they have discovered that they get more by keeping silent,' Mother went on.

'Of course we don't know how cunning the man who taught them was,' said Granny reflectively. 'But there is something unusual about them. They haven't even used the beggar's jingle.'

'Whatever is the beggar's jingle?' I asked.

'It's a jingle that all beggars know,' said Granny. 'It is as old as India itself. Every beggar-boy learns it from his father. They say: "Baksheesh, swami, baksheesh, no father, no mother, many small brothers and sisters, baksheesh, baksheesh." '

'Doesn't a beggar-boy ever have a father or mother?' I asked.

'Of course he has, very often. But his father teaches him to lie so that people will feel sorry for him,' answered Granny. 'I have heard, too, that in big cities there are men who make their living by stealing children from their parents and teaching them to beg. These children get plenty of beatings and nothing to eat until they have learnt the jingle.'

Mother looked quickly round for Kitto. Where was he now? Children could be stolen in a town. But luckily he had merely become bored by our conversation and had gone over to the railway: he was sitting there piling little heaps of stones on the rails again.

We spent the rest of the day in the same place. Trains came and went, there was something happening all the time. Father sat in the shade, smoking. He never moved, but his eyes followed everything that went on. The bullock was grazing and Kempi lay chewing the cud beside the cart. The beggar-boy had fallen asleep with his back against the trunk of a palm tree, and the girl was sleeping with her head in his lap. Now and then Kitto ran down to the shining rails, but each time Mother called him back.

Towards nightfall Granny milked Kempi. She put half the

milk in a clean pan and then took me with her to the station platform. Granny held out the pan of milk in front of her, but everyone was much too busy to look at us, so we went into the big building. As soon as we came through the door, a young woman got up from her place on the floor. She had been nursing her youngest child while three others stood around her whimpering.

'Is your milk clean and is there any water in it, mother?' she asked.

'See for yourself,' said Granny, and held out the pan.

'It looks good. How much do you want for it?' she asked again.

'Two annas,' said Granny, for the price of milk in the town was twice as high as in our village.

'Give me what you have, mother,' said the young woman, and held out a tin bowl. At the same time she fished a coin out of a little bag she carried on her arm. That was the first time I saw a woman carry money.

When we came back to the others, Granny said quite calmly to Father:

'Perhaps I had better keep the money we get for the milk. One day we must take Shanta to the bazaar with us, and there are various things we shall need to buy now that she is soon to be married.'

Father grumbled a little, but let Granny keep the money. All the rules were being so completely upset on this journey that I could hardly believe it was true.

By now it was almost dark. In the front and the back of the big white building the new bright light was lit. Inside it was still day; outside under our palm trees the night had come. But every time a train went by, our little domain was also bathed in light. We made a fire of some rice-straw, a few twigs and a

58

cow-cake, to cook our rice. When it was cooked, we ate it with some sour milk.

The two little strangers sat watching us in silence. Mother tried to talk to them but they didn't answer. Now and then they whispered to each other. They could speak, then. Perhaps they used a different language?

'Come and get a little rice, you two,' she called, but they didn't move. She ladled out a handful of rice on to a leaf, and I went over and laid it in front of the boy. Once again he pressed his forehead against my foot.

As soon as I had gone back to the fire, he divided the portion of rice into two equal parts with his right hand, and this time they ate it at once in the shelter of the darkness.

Mother washed the cooking-pot at the water-pipe in the wall. There was a bright light just above it. She brought some water back with her so that Father could rinse his mouth and his hands after the meal. The rest of us went over to the pipe ourselves and washed. It was like suddenly going from night into day: when we came back to the night again, Mother was unrolling the sleeping-mat among the palm trees.

We lay close together, with part of our clothing pulled up over our heads. Kempi and the bullock were munching nearby and that gave us a comfortable feeling of security. When a train went by, I saw that the two children were sitting close together with their backs against the farthest palm tree. Perhaps they really had no other place to sleep in. It was getting chilly; in the morning, when the sun rose, it would be cold. They hadn't a stitch of clothing on their bodies. Surely they would soon go home to their mother and the sleeping-mat? Perhaps she was very, very poor, but she must be somewhere. If only Granny hadn't told us about those people in the big cities who stole children to make beggars of them.

When at length I fell asleep that night, I dreamt that the black snake came gliding up to me and said: 'Child, where is my milk? I am thirsty. Child, have you left the village for good?'

I woke with the earth shaking and a loud noise roaring above me. I sat up bewildered. 'Is that rain, Granny?'

'No, no, Shanta,' said Granny, pulling her sari from her head, 'that is a train. You are not at home in the village.'

Now it all came back to me: the journey, the town, the railway station and the trains going and coming.

The others were waking up. I longed for the village, and crept close to Granny.

'Let us go home today, Granny,' I whispered. 'Get Father to take us home.'

'Whatever for, Shanta?' Granny whispered back.

'The town is horrible, Granny. I never want to leave the village again.'

'You aren't properly awake, my child,' said Granny soothingly, stroking my hair. 'The day hasn't begun.'

The sleeping-mat was wet with dew. Our clothes were damp and we were all rather cold. The sun was still too low to warm the earth and dry up the dew. Father got up and went into the big building; Mother sat up, and it was she who first thought about the two little strangers. They were still there, asleep on the bare ground. The boy lay with one hand under his cheek and the other holding fast to the girl who was leaning against him.

'Poor little things,' said Mother, 'they have no home.'

'No,' said Granny, 'not even a place to go to at night.'

Mother went up to the children. 'Come, let us move them on to the mat,' she said, and bent down to pick up the girl. But the moment Mother's hand touched her, both she and the boy were

60

wide awake. They huddled closer but otherwise didn't move: they just stared at us with frightened eyes.

'Come and sleep on the mat,' invited Mother, but they gave no sign that they had understood.

'Come,' whispered Granny softly, patting the mat with her hands as she spoke. Both children stood up. The boy looked at Granny but shook his head. Then he took the girl's hand and again they stood gazing at us in silence.

'There is something that makes these children more frightened of people than beggar children usually are,' said Granny.

'They don't beg,' said Mother, 'they just look at us.'

'Leave them in peace while we go over to the water-pipe and wash ourselves,' said Granny.

Mother looked round for Kitto. He was already sitting by the railway, piling stones on the rails. She called him, and when we came to the water-pipe, she took off his shirt, and let him run underneath the water. The rest of us washed our hands and faces, smoothed our hair and arranged our saris.

The strange children had followed us. They had left their basket under the palm trees.

As soon as we were ready, we walked over to the railway again. When we were half way, Granny looked back cautiously at the children.

'Don't turn around,' she said, 'they are washing themselves. The girl is right underneath the water. He is washing her all over.'

When we had eaten our breakfast, they came back. Their skin was clean and warm with rubbing and they had tried to smooth their hair with their hands.

Granny had a piece of comb. She sat down on the mat and tried to call the girl to her. The child hid behind the boy, but he took her hand and led her to Granny. At first she was frightened,

61

but gradually she became quiet and allowed Granny to comb her hair. This took some while, for it was a long time since it had been done, and Granny caught many tiny creatures in it. When at last it hung in a fine plait down her back, the little girl smiled happily. The boy's hair was combed too; it was curly and reached to his shoulders.

Father wouldn't leave the station that day either.

'We women will go and sell the cakes of cow-dung then,' said Granny. 'Kitto must stay here. He is too little to walk a long way among all these crowds.'

Where was Kitto? Down by the railway lines again, piling up the stones. Mother said anxiously:

'He is always down by those rails. If only he remembers to run away when a train comes.'

'Women are always worrying,' grumbled Father, 'the boy will be all right.' So mother could say no more.

'We will take Kempi with us,' said Granny, 'she hasn't been milked this morning. Perhaps we shall find someone who will buy her milk.'

'See that she doesn't do any damage,' said Father.

Mother untied Kempi from the palm tree. Granny set the basket of cow-dung cakes on her head and walked in front. She was not really tall herself, but the round pile of cakes on her head would be seen high above the people and the carts and the cars. Mother followed close behind her with Kempi. The cow had a rope round her neck and I held fast to it.

When we had crossed the square in front of the big building, I discovered that the two strange children were just behind us.

They were hand in hand and were not carrying the bamboo basket. They were talking quietly together, but using words I didn't understand.

We all followed Granny as best we could, down the narrow street where as usual there were so many people that you had to thread your way through them. At the first corner, we turned away from the crowd and came into a street without shops. There were white houses on both sides, and they were tall and had balconies like my uncle's house.

'This is where the rich people live,' said Granny, looking round her.

'They are high caste, too,' said Mother.

'Perhaps,' said Granny 'but it's not certain. Caste is not as important here as it is in our village. In a town, what you need is money.'

'If you are a brahmin you are rich too,' said Mother.

'No, in a town a brahmin isn't always rich,' answered Granny. 'Here, the richest men are the merchants. I think we are in the street where the merchants live.'

The two children were keeping very close to us as if they feared some danger or other.

'Look at those children,' said Mother, 'they know this place. They are certainly used to being driven away.'

'I think this is the right place for us to sell our goods in,' said Granny. 'It's lucky we have Kempi with us and that she is decked out so finely. Anyone can see we are respectable people.'

Granny walked quickly up to a house and knocked on the door. She squatted down by the doorstep, lifted the basket from her head and placed it beside her.

The door was opened, and a woman in a green sari with a gleaming border came out. She had a large diamond in her nose, heavy rings in her ears, and many bracelets. The foot which showed beneath her sari had a ring on every toe. As she stepped forward, we greeted her by raising both hands with palms pressed together to our foreheads, and bowing low. Naturally we had first carefully pulled our saris across our mouths. Granny said:

'Greetings, lady. We have brought dry dung-cakes from our village. It you will pick them up you will see that I am right.'

The woman picked up one of the cakes. 'Is there any earth mixed in it, mother?' she said.

'Pick up another and judge for yourself, lady,' answered Granny.

'The weight is what it ought to be, and that's a fine cow you have,' said the woman, 'but who are these others with you?'

'My daughter-in-law and her daughter,' answered Granny.

'And why aren't your daughter-in-law's two youngest children wearing any clothes?' asked the woman.

Granny was silent for a moment. She didn't want to say that the little ones didn't belong to us, so she answered:

'We shall buy clothes when we have sold the dung-cakes, lady.'

'What is your price?' asked the woman.

Granny asked the price that my uncle had told us was paid in the town, and the woman didn't try to beat her down. She took almost half the cakes in the basket. and paid with coins from a little bag which she kept under her sarı. Granny bit the coins and tied them in a corner of her sari before she bowed to the woman again. Then she put the basket on her head, stood up, and walked on.

We all followed her. A little farther down the street, she knocked on another door and sat outside it in the same way as before. The woman who came out was carrying a child on her hip, and two older children were peeping from behind her sari.

Once again, Granny recommended the cow-dung cakes, but the woman asked: 'Where do you come from, mother?'

'From a village on the other side of the river, three days' journey away,' answered Granny.

'Have you sturdy children in your village?' asked the woman.

'Sturdy children and healthy cows,' answered Granny.

The woman looked at Kempi, saying:

'Does your cow give more milk than your children can drink?'

'We are poor peasants,' answered Granny, 'my children don't drink milk every day.'

'What is the price of your milk?' asked the woman.

Granny named the price that the woman at the station had paid.

'The price is high,' was the answer, 'but if I can see you milk the cow, I will pay it. The milk must have no water in it.' She went into the house and fetched a bowl.

Kempi made no fuss about being milked in the middle of the street As the woman gave Granny the money, she said: 'May your children and your children's children always be strong and healthy,' and then she went into the house with the milk.

We found it just as easy to sell the rest of the cow-dung cakes, and before the sun stood so high that the houses cast no shadow, we had finished. Granny had the money in her sari. I didn't know how much it was, and it never occurred to me that she would dare to use it without Father's permission.

There we stood, in the middle of the street in the big city. It was so early in the day that there was no need to return to the station yet, but where should we go? Granny said:

'Let us see if we can find the bazaar.'

'Oh yes,' said Mother, 'let's go to the bazaar.'

'Bazaar,' said the boy suddenly, and pointed to the narrow street we had come from.

'Of course the children will know the town,' said Granny, 'and "bazaar" must be a word that is found in all the languages of India. He will show us the way.'

The children had already started to walk back in the direction from which we had come. The boy turned round to see whether we were following. We did so, and Mother said:

'You can see he is proud to be the one who leads the way.'

We made our way through the crowds in the narrow street. Mother led Kempi and I held fast to the halter round her neck. The children took us through some little alleys where the houses were so close together that there was hardly room for me to walk at Kempi's side. At length we went along what seemed like a gutter stained with betel-juice, red as blood. Ragged men and women sat on every doorstep: many of them looked ill. There was one man who had lost both his feet. He had bound sacks round his knees, and when he saw us, he rolled forward on to his hands and crawled after us crying, 'Baksheesh, baksheesh.'

Kempi was terrified, and the rest of us felt very ill at ease. Even the children looked frightened. The boy took hold of Kempi's rope to hurry us along.

'I wonder why they have brought us here?' said Mother. 'There's something they are afraid of.'

'It's probably a short cut to the bazaar,' said Granny, 'and it's broad daylight, so what could happen?'

We reached a wider street; luckily this was a perfectly ordinary street like most of the others in the town. There were shops along both sides of it. They were close together and all of them were open-fronted. We could see right inside to all the fine things on the shelves.

Our earlier feeling of uneasiness vanished, and we walked more and more slowly so that we could look at everything. At length Mother and Kempi came to a halt at a place where so many saris hung in front of a shop that the opening was almost covered. Mother went so close that Granny said:

'Mind the cow, Kamala. She mustn't touch anything. Perhaps the shopkeepers won't like a cow so close to their goods.'

Just in front of us lay another cow, peacefully chewing the cud in the midst of the traffic. She appeared to be quite alone without anyone to look after her.

'No one is driving that one away,' said Mother.

'No, but that's a city cow who is used to being here every day. Kempi looks as if she might get up to something with all these people around her.'

And true enough there was fear in Kempi's eyes. I turned her head a little so that she could see the other cow which was lying in the dust. Perhaps it would soothe her to see it, and perhaps it would please her if she understood that she herself was much finer.

The man in the shop came out and began to hold his saris up for us to see. 'Lovely wedding saris, lovely wedding saris, lady – come in and see them, lady. My saris are very very cheap, lady, very very cheap.'

He held up a heavy blue sari. It had white lotus flowers in the corner, and a broad white stripe across it. It was made of cotton, and was much more beautiful than any sari Mother or Granny had ever had. It must certainly be very expensive. What would Granny say? It was to her the man was talking.

'Feel how heavy the material is, lady. Look at the colour. You like pretty colours. Your cow is decorated with gay colours for the festival. You have a fine cow and lovely daughters.'

67

The man couldn't have seen me, for I knew quite well that I was dark and plain. Granny quietly cut short his flow of words, saying:

'Haven't you a lighter-coloured sari? Can't you see that my daughter is dark?'

At once the man found a sari that was the colour of a pink lotus. There were many bright colours in the border and it was light and shimmering. I didn't dare to look at Granny, but I heard her say: 'What is your price?'

The man named a price that was higher than the pay for a month's work in the rice fields. I knew then that it was not for me.

'Your price is too high,' said Granny, 'we are poor peasants.'

'Poor peasants sometimes have money tied up in their saris,' said the man.

'Your price is too high,' repeated Granny, and began to walk away. We followed her. The man shouted a lower price after us, and then, as we continued to walk on, a still lower one.

'Never mind, Shanta,' said Granny, 'perhaps we'll come back tomorrow.'

Farther down the street was the entrance to the bazaar. It was a high gateway almost like the great door into the railway station. There were bars across it so that people could edge their way in, but it was impossible for a cow to get through. The boy understood that we couldn't all leave Kempi: he took the rope from Mother's hand, tied it tightly to the bars, and stood beside Kempi to show that we could go in. I was a little uneasy. Supposing he made off with Kempi while we were gone? She and the children could easily disappear in the throng. I said nothing about this, but Granny must have understood what I was thinking for she said:

'You need not be afraid, Shanta, he will look after her. They won't go off anywhere, I'm sure of that.'

Mother was already making her way into the bazaar.

'We must go in now,' continued Granny. 'it will never do to get separated. It's just the time of day when the crowds are thickest.'

Mother stopped in front of a stall with gaudy bracelets and all kinds of glittering things. I had never seen a shop like it. The wall at the back was hung with mirrors great and small.

'You'll get a mirror from your husband on your wedding-day,' said Mother. 'Mine is broken!'

Above and below the mirrors, and everywhere on the walls, were bright-coloured flowers.

'They are made of paper,' said Granny, 'they have no scent. The townsfolk use them to pay honour to the gods.'

In one of the topmost corners I caught sight of a picture of the goddess of beauty, Lakshmi. Wearing a pink sari, she rose from an enormous lotus flower of the same colour. Under the lotus flower was a bundle of burnt-out incense-sticks.

The woman who sold these things was beautifully dressed in a sari with flowers all over it. Her thick black hair shone with oil, and there were fresh white flowers in the coil at the nape of her neck. Granny had gone close to her and stood staring, saying nothing. I crept up to her too and whispered: 'How lovely she is, Granny.'

'She has put a lot of paint on her face,' Granny whispered back.

I had thought that she had been born with a light skin. In our village the women painted their faces too. They all used cumcum for the red spot on their foreheads, put yellow on the lower part of their cheeks, and a heavy black line round their eyes. Even the children had this from the time they were three or four years old.

This woman was painted in a quite different way. She had full, red lips and pale cheeks.

'Come and buy my cumcum, lady,' she said, 'it's the finest in the bazaar and very cheap.'

But Granny was silent. She was usually self-assured with strangers; now it almost seemed as if she were a little afraid of the woman, or were her eyes held by all the glittering bracelets which hung side by side on two bamboo sticks across the whole shop ? She raised her hand slowly and pointed to where they sparkled most brightly.

The bracelets were very light and thin, not at all like those the silversmith in our village made. His were silver and had the hues of silver, but these shone and glittered in all possible colours.

The woman took a handful and passed them over to us. All three of us were staring at them now.

'You won't find finer wedding ornaments, lady,' she said.

When Granny got a closer view of them she became her usual calm self again.

'They are not real ornaments, they're new-fangled city trash,' she muttered. Aloud, she asked:

'What is your price ?'

'Six for two annas, lady,' said the woman. Granny quickly produced the money and took the bracelets which had been offered to her. She shared them out, three to Mother and three to me.

'You must have a bracelet too,' said Mother, and wanted to give her one back.

'They are not for me,' said Granny, pushing her hand away, 'they are for you while you are young. When my husband was alive, I had ornaments. Now I am old, I don't need them.' We hurried on, but I kept looking at my wrist which glittered more brightly than Kempi's horns.

The bazaar was a big place with all kinds of stalls and shops, most of which were covered with palm-leaf mats as a protection against the sun. The stalls stood in rows along narrow streets. In one street you could buy fruit: oranges, lemons, bananas and mangoes lay in heaps on the ground, and there were many other kinds of which I didn't know the name. In another street there were vegetables which didn't grow in our village, and all sorts of spices.

There were rice, ground-nuts, sugar-cane and oil, pictures of the gods, incense-sticks, bamboo baskets and jugs. A whole street was given up to stalls that sold leather sandals. There were so many sandals that there must have been a pair for every man and woman in the world.

'The world is vast,' said Granny. 'There are not even enough sandals here for all the people in our own country, and most of them go barefoot as we do.'

Beside the street of sandals was one where material was sold. There was coarse cotton for the shirts and trousers that men wear for work in the rice fields and there was the cheapest kind of sari.

Half way down the street, Granny suddenly stopped and said:

'We'll buy some clothes for the children. We are poor enough, and from time to time we go hungry like most other people, but those two are all alone in the world. They are cold at night.'

To think that that had never come into my head when Granny bought the bracelets! I didn't need them, but I had forgotten that because they glittered so. I began to pull them off: perhaps we could exchange them for clothing for the children.

'Keep the bracelets,' said Granny. 'If your father gives us leave to buy your wedding sari in the town, we'll find a way to save a little of the money.' As usual Granny had a solution for every problem.

We bought a coarse loin-cloth for the boy and a little piece of material for the girl. Mother would make her a skirt.

The sun was high in the sky now, and the bazaar was no longer crowded. The traders began to spread mats over their goods. We went towards the exit. There was no sign of Kempi, but when we came right out into the street, we found her and the children a little farther on beside a house. She was lying chewing the cud with her back against the wall, and the children were asleep, leaning against her. The boy had tied her rope round his wrist.

We went to them and woke them. As quick as lightning, the boy raised his arm to shield his face as if he feared a blow, but when he realized who it was, he smiled shyly and quickly untied Kempi's rope.

Granny had kept her hands behind her back. Now she produced the clothes, first the loin-cloth. The boy stared. He obviously couldn't believe his own eyes and he made no move to take it. Granny shook it out and tied it round his waist. Then he understood, and threw himself to the ground, pressing his forehead against her feet. She couldn't stop him. Mother tied the piece of stuff round the girl's shoulders to show her that there was something for her too.

This performance must have bored Kempi because she had got up and was walking up the street by herself.

'I think she has an idea of the direction we should take,' said Granny.

The boy hurried after her and took hold of her rope, and the girl darted after him to take his hand.

'They look happy enough now,' said Mother. 'If only we could understand what they are talking about.'

There were not many people to be seen, for it was time to rest in the shade, but a man came striding towards us on the other side of the street. His coat was the colour of a ripe orange, and it swung about his legs because he was walking fast. He looked neither to the right nor to the left, but as he went by I knew that it was the yogi with the cold eyes.

Fortunately he didn't see us, and immediately afterwards he turned into the narrow alley that the boy had led us through on the way to the bazaar.

Suddenly we realized that the children had gone. Kempi was ambling along with the rope trailing behind her.

'What has become of the children?' said Mother.

'I kept my eyes on the yogi because I thought I knew him,' said Granny, 'and now the children have disappeared. Something or other must have frightened them.'

'Well, they must be somewhere,' said Mother. 'Where can they have hidden themselves in this short time? Here there are only shops with closed shutters and an open street.'

But there was something Mother hadn't noticed. There were two long flights of steps from the street up to each shop. Beneath the steps there was a cavity, and from one of these the scared and dirty children now crawled out. The boy tried to brush the worst of the dust from his loin-cloth, and the girl pulled her piece of stuff tightly round her. They went quickly up to Kempi, and hurried on with her through another street to the station. We almost had to run to keep up with them.

That morning, two more families from our village had arrived. They had encamped by the railway not far from us. Now the men were sitting under the palm trees and chatting idly to Father, Kitto was making his heaps of stones on the rails, and on the station, people were sleeping among boxes and bundles.

We settled down and dozed by the side of the cart. The children sat near us but at a good distance from the men.

Towards nightfall, we went over to the women to hear the

village news. They asked us about life in the city, and admired our bracelets. Mother and Granny described the village by the dam, and my uncle's fine house, and his sons who were studying in the town. It wasn't said in so many words, but everyone understood that perhaps a husband had been found for me.

Before the rainy season, I had been terribly embarrassed when anyone spoke of marriage. Now it was different: I was obliged to be the centre of the gathering, and ornaments and saris were discussed until it was time to cook the rice.

The evening passed like the evenings in our village. The men talked together under the palm trees about money and politics. Father was so absorbed that he didn't notice that the children were wearing clothes. He didn't say anything either when we let them sleep that night on the rice-straw in the bottom of the cart.

For nine days we lived like this by the railway. Mother, Granny and I ate a little less rice than usual, so that every time there was something left for the children.

We women went to the shopping streets every day, and occasionally to the bazaar. Father went with us only once. A diamond was bought for me and inserted in my nose instead of the little piece of wood. When we came home that evening, I felt very grown-up among the other women. They turned me round and round to see the stone from every side, and afterwards they talked for a long time about its price and quality. My only regret was that the old woman from my uncle's house wasn't there to see me.

Saris were bought too, not the beautiful lotus-coloured one, nor the heavy blue one with the white border, but an ordinary reddish-brown wedding sari with yellow stripes, and two other saris for work in the house and in the field. The proper wedding ornaments – a silver belt decorated with small round balls, bracelets and anklets – would be made by the silversmith in our own village.

'No one shall say of us that we think more highly of the town than of our village,' said Granny. 'The silversmith at home will not cheat us over the weight of the silver we pay for.'

One evening when we came home from the bazaar, Father was not there. The children were sitting under the palm trees and Kitto was down by the railway lines. Mother was very concerned at seing him there when no grown-up was at hand. What might happen if the train came without his realizing it? The other women told us that the men had gone to a coffee-house in the narrow street to hear what the townsmen talked about.

'That's odd,' said Granny, 'my son doesn't usually spend money on such things.'

'Let's slip down there to see where it is,' said Mother.

She and Granny took Kitto between them and I followed, but the children remained where they were, perhaps to keep an eye on Kempi.

The coffee-house was half-way down the narrow street. Outside was a stall where cigarettes were sold. A few beggars sat on the pavement, and the steps were covered with red betel-juice. We went as close to the entrance as we dared, and cautiously peeped in, when someone went through the curtain. Inside in the semi-darkness, men were sitting on benches round the tables. Each one had a coffee cup in front of him, and took a sip from time to time. Many of them were smoking, others were only talking. It was almost like harvest time in our village, but nobody was playing cards, and it didn't look as if anyone was drinking palm spirit.

Father was talking eagerly with the men who sat near him; he never talked like that to us at home. Mother and Granny seemed to be relieved by what they saw.

'No palm spirit and no cards,' said Mother.

'Of course my son must be there when men are exchanging words of wisdom about serious matters,' said Granny.

We didn't stay there long, for it was not a place that women came to, and Father and the men from the village must not see us. By the time they returned, we had long ago settled down on the sleeping-mat, but even longer we lay listening to them as they went on talking under the palm trees.

The following evening the men went to the coffee-house again. When they had gone, Granny said:

'Let us go to the palace and see the lights being lit.'

'Dare we do that?' asked Mother. 'They are not lit until some time after sunset. Can we go alone in the dark to a place we don't know?'

'The way to the palace is through the narrow street, and then along the wide one with all the shops,' said Granny. 'Both are well lighted as soon as the sun goes down. It's as bright as day.'

Mother allowed herself to be persuaded. She and Granny took Kitto by the hand, and off we went. As usual, the children gave no sign of wanting to leave our camp under the palm trees in the evening. They had already crept into the rice-straw in the bottom of the cart. The boy looked after us with watchful eyes.

'It's a good thing we have him there,' said Granny. 'He's used to the darkness and will keep an eye on the animals while we are away.'

When we came to the open space at the end of the wide street, Mother was really afraid of the darkness on the other side.

76

'Let's go back,' she said, 'the darkness has completely hidden the palace. It can hide many other things too. Come, let's go back.'

'No,' said Granny, 'you know the square by day. You know it is quite flat and of red trampled earth. You know it stretches from here right up to the palace. You know that there is a park on both sides of it, and that the maharajah's soldiers stand on guard all round it. There is nothing to be afraid of.'

'It may be that the darkness doesn't hide anything dangerous,' said Mother, 'but all the same I am afraid to go into it when we are alone.'

'We are not alone,' retorted Granny, 'don't you see how many village folk are going by us into the darkness the whole time? They are sitting in the square and waiting for the town clock to strike seven, for then all the lights will go on.'

Mother let herself be persuaded once more and we went into the dark square. But we had not gone far before she gave a little frightened cry. She had stumbled against something in the dark. Kitto whimpered, and pulled at Granny to make her go back, but she said:

'Just stand still for a moment, all three of you, and when your eyes are accustomed to the darkness you will see that the square is full of people who are sitting and waiting.'

We stood still. Before our eyes the darkness changed from black to grey, and the grey was full of dark, silent figures which covered the square right up to the palace. What Mother had stumbled against was a little group of women and children who sat huddled together.

'Come,' said Granny, as she began to grope her way carefully through the many little groups of people, 'let us get nearer to the palace.'

We held each other by the hand and crept silently forward.

At length Granny stopped at a place where there was just room for us all to sit on the warm ground. It was impossible to see how big the crowd was, but the evening air smelt of humanity. Now and then a low-toned remark was heard in the darkness, and so great was the silence that the sound carried a long way.

The town clock began to strike seven. 'Now it will happen,' said Granny.

Almost as she spoke, light flooded the whole of the front of the palace. It was so strong that its beam reached even those who sat farthest back in the square. I had seen the palace in the daytime, and it was big and beautiful with its domes and spires, as Granny called them, but that night it was lovelier than any castle described in our country's holy book that Granny could have told me about.

Each light shone like a star, and they clustered thicker than blossoms on a gulmohar tree. In the midst of all this light sat the maharajah on his balcony. The moment that he appeared, a murmur ran through the thousands of people gathered there.

'May the gods protect our country's good and noble father,' murmured Granny.

'Is he one of the gods?' I whispered.

'Don't ask such questions, child,' answered Granny, 'it is not for us to say what he is.'

We were a long way away from the balcony, but all the same we could see him clearly in the beam of light: the gold in his turban, the silk his clothes were made of, the diamonds and the other precious stones that sparkled on his fingers.

Did he live quite alone in that huge house, or did he dwell with the gods? He looked more like a god than a man. It seemed too, as if he had great power over all those who were sitting in the square in front of him. Mother and Granny sat stock still, staring at the palace with wide-open eyes. There was deep silence over the whole crowd, and not a single person moved.

Cautiously, I turned my head to see what was behind me: dark saris and white cloths around motionless brown faces. As far as my eyes could see in the darkness, people were sitting in rows.

But there, not far from us, one man was standing on his feet. He was a yogi; the light fell on his orange coat and on his face. He was looking at us, and not at the palace. Why was he doing this? Did he know us? I shivered a little at the thought. The warm darkness suddenly felt as cold as morning mist. I was glad that we should soon be on our way home to the village.

Quickly I turned my head again. Granny had said that tomorrow was the day of the great parade and after that we should go home. Kitto was asleep now with his head in Mother's lap, and for the rest of the time I sat motionless like the grown-up people.

When the town clock struck again, the light went out. The hour when the divine one showed himself to his people was over. Everyone stood up, and now we had to be careful to keep together in the tumult that broke out in the darkness, as each family hurried to its sleeping-place somewhere or other in the town.

There was great activity in the stables where the maharajah's elephants were kept. The great white male elephant was being washed and adorned for the festival. On his massive legs huge fantastic flowers were painted in yellow and green, and his toenails were carefully gilded. The triangular ornament studded with precious stones was polished and inspected. This was no small task, for the ornament was big enough to cover his entire forehead and part of his trunk. The red velvet cloth, which was to be spread beneath the maharajah's throne on the elephant's back, was cleaned and brushed.

Beside him stood the two dark brown jungle elephants. Pink lotus flowers were painted on their forelegs, and dancing cobras on their hind legs. Their youngest baby, a mischievous little fellow, was capering about and teasing the keepers. He was to be painted exactly like his parents, and in the parade the three of them were to walk behind the big white elephant. For several days the keepers had tried to make him walk in step with the old ones, round and round in the elephant-house. It would be a scandal indeed if the forest giants suddenly broke out of the procession and trampled on the onlookers, and the little one might make them do this.

The big white elephant was very displeased that the jungle elephants were to take part in his procession, for it *was* his. No doubt the people thought that the maharajah, the divine one, was the all-important person, but he knew better. Had he not carried three maharajahs in many harvest processions ? Through the years he had seen the rulers' power and wealth decrease. The maharajah still had a massive gold howdah with a silk canopy to set upon his back, but how long would he be able to keep it! In these modern days, a maharajah's position had become very insecure. No, the only members of the procession this year who were really worthy of honour were himself and the ancient sacred cow belonging to the palace. Could any other elephant in the palace move a foot as slowly as he could, and could any other cow be as steady as she was ?

Now, however, the maharajah had had the deplorable idea that a pair of dark brown jungle elephants and their impertinent offspring should walk behind him in the procession. It was an insult. There was no knowing what these uncivilized creatures might do. Yesterday, for example, in the elephant house, that little fellow had come up to him and said:

'The skin of your head and nose is as pink as a lotus. Are you ill?'

Ill, indeed! It was just because he looked different from every other elephant that the young maharajah's grandfather had chosen him for the place of honour in the procession, and no one had ever had cause to complain of him. However loudly the people along the route shouted 'Long live our divine father!' waving in front of his ears every possible kind of contraption that makes a noise, he never faltered. He never got out of step. The maharajah on his back ran no risk of losing face by a sudden movement of the howdah.

A door in the palace was opened. A servant came running out with the news that the astrologer had just said that the best time for the procession to start would be at four minutes past four that same afternoon.

The activity became feverish. The old sacred cow had her hooves and horns gilded. The ancient cloth with all the golden bells on it was tried on, though everyone knew that it fitted her. She had worn it every year since she was young. The elephant wondered whether she knew that her place immediately behind him in the procession had been taken by the jungle elephants.

After the noonday rest, the procession was formed up outside the palace. With bowed head, swaying his huge body to and fro on his solid legs, the elephant stood and waited. These human ants were so busy: had they enough memory and forethought to get everything in its right order?

First the drummers, who were to give the procession a festive rhythm. After them, various regiments of the maharajah's soldiers in glittering uniforms. Then a group of riflemen on white horses, and following them another group on black ones. Nobody remembered the elephant, but he remembered himself, and went and took his place of his own accord. That set everybody going in earnest. The howdah hadn't been fetched from the treasury, and where was the man with the key?

He was found with astonishing speed, and the howdah was brought. The elephant had to kneel while it was lifted up and secured to his back. The high white steps on the small red wheels were pushed into position, so that the maharajah could use them to reach the howdah.

Two keepers came out, leading the jungle elephants. The cheeky little fellow kept between his parents' legs and it was as well he did, for the big white elephant looked dangerous.

'If he comes within reach of my trunk, I'll pick him up and throw him over the hedge into the park,' he thought, 'and if he gets too near me during the parade, there'll be an accident.'

After the jungle elephants, the cow took her place in the ranks, and after that came the great silver coach that the maharajah had been given by his father after his long journey to the countries of the West. From that journey he brought back the thoughts and customs of the West to the palace, and he began to dress like a Westerner. But he still kept to the old ways in the harvest procession.

The rest of the parade was a mixture of war-chariots, huntsmen, horsemen with leopard-skins over their backs, policemen, and all the costly palanquins and coaches that were to be found in the palace. When the whole procession had formed up, it reached twice round the palace.

At last the moment had come. The town clock struck four, the palace doors opened and the maharajah came out. All the gold and precious stones of the treasury adorned his white silk garments. He was worthy to sit on the throne on the elephant's back. He cast his eyes over the procession and remarked to the master of ceremonies:

'Western rulers often drive in a car in processions like this. It would be easier for me to do that too. Perhaps the old white elephant could be harnessed to a car.'

The elephant raised his truck. Harnessed to a car! That must be worse than having a tiger behind you. This was the modern age, then. He had already heard that the maharajah had seven times as many cars as an elephant has toenails.

The master of ceremonies' hands trembled as he raised them in salutation. Then he bowed low before his ruler and said:

'Your Highness, the gods and the people like the howdah and the old elephant better than a car.'

Only those who stood nearest heard the maharajah mutter: 'But I, the divine one, prefer a car.'

As in former years, the maharajah strode across the square, mounted the white steps and took his place in the howdah on the elephant's back. At the second when the clock showed four minutes past four, everything was ready. The master of ceremonies gave a signal to the drummers, and the procession moved off.

First it went up the wide street and past the great temple. It turned into the narrow street, passed the railway station and the park, and at length went in the direction of the spring at the foot of the mountain. Its goal was the sacred tree.

All along the route rows and rows of people stood as they were accustomed to do. They sat on balconies and rooftops and shouted:

'Long live His Highness, our good and divine ruler!'

The girl Shanta and her family stood just at the point where the narrow street opens on to the station square.

We had been there since the morning. For once, Father wanted to be in everything. The moment we were awake he had said:

'Today we must tie up the animals and hide our things away so that they are out of sight. Today we will all see His Highness's procession.'

Everything had been put in order, and Granny said:

'Let's take one of the coconuts with us and then we shan't be hungry or thirsty if the day is hot.'

Without a word, Father took his sickle and cut the top off a nut. He carefully put the top on again and tied a cloth round it: Mother carried the nut under her sari all day.

Granny had been down to the big building to wash out the cooking-pot. When she came back she said:

'People are already gathering in the square to see His Highness. Let us go at once.'

On the corner of the narrow street, Father saw a doorstep that jutted further out than the others. We sat down on it.

'Perhaps somebody will come and stand in front of us,' said Mother.

'They will be sent away when the procession comes because the street is so narrow here,' answered Father.

'We shall be quite near to His Highness,' said Granny with satisfaction.

The children sat silently behind us, but Kitto kept wanting to run back to the railway.

Before the sun was overhead the station square was full. Rows of people were squatting in front of the houses in the narrow street. Most of them were dozing. The sun was burning and there wasn't a spot of shade. The step we sat on was higher than the others near it, so that we had a good view of everything.

Late in the afternoon we heard music down in the town. It came nearer. Men on horseback came and moved the people who were sitting too far out in the street.

Now we saw the first drummers. People stood up. I stepped forward to see better.

'Be careful,' said Granny, 'it has happened before that a horse or an elephant in the procession has turned savage. Don't let yourself be trampled on.'

Mother caught hold of Kitto protectively, and the next moment the first soldiers were right in front of us. But my eyes were caught by something that shone and glittered farther down the street. It was a golden howdah. High above the crowd, it swayed slowly nearer on the back of a huge white elephant.

'It is His Highness,' said Father, 'in the howdah made of gold.'

'Look, Shanta! Look, Kamala!' said Granny excitedly.

'Long live His Highness, our divine ruler!' shouted Father with everybody else.

The yellow and green flowers on the elephant's legs were quite close to us. They were taller than a man.

'The old elephant looks dangerous,' whispered Granny.

'Look out, it can't stand the little brown one behind it,' said Mother.

The little elephant reached with his trunk for the big one's tail.

'Let's hope there won't be an accident,' wailed a woman beside us.

'Long live His Highness, our divine ruler!' shouted Father and the others again.

The big white elephant had almost come to a halt. He blocked the whole street. Slowly his trunk rose in the air, like a cobra rearing. What was going to happen? He began to swing his head from side to side. His trunk waved above those who stood nearest. He lifted one enormous foot. The great yellow-green flower came nearer and was planted in a group of people just behind Father. Kitto shrieked, but by a miracle nobody was beneath the foot. People threw themselves out of the way in wild confusion. The frightened maharajah looked around him.

Then one of the keepers noticed the little brown elephant, ran up to him and gave him a rap over the trunk. Quickly the young one drew back between his parents. The big white elephant shook his trunk disdainfully, stood quite still for a moment and then walked on, slowly and majestically as before.

The maharajah's sacred cow waddled past us, fat and lazy. She gleamed with gold and her bells rang, but she wasn't as young and handsome as Kempi.

When the whole procession had gone by, the crowd started to break up. Some followed it, others went home. When the maharajah had bathed in the spring and sacrificed to the gods under the sacred tree, they would all come back here again. Father decided that we should sit and wait for them.

Mother took the top off the coconut and we drank the milk. Father broke the shell into pieces, and used the top to scrape out the soft white flesh so that we could eat it. Boys went through the crowd with sugar cakes on flat trays. Father gave Granny permission to buy one for each of us. We ate slowly, enjoying every crumb of the unaccustomed sweetmeats.

The sun had set and night had fallen over the town when the

procession came back. The crowds who followed it carried torches, and there was shouting and screaming and jostling in the gleam of the flickering lights. We were pushed back against the house wall and strangers separated us from each other.

When at length the hubbub had subsided, I was quite alone. All the others had gone. I didn't like it: everybody seemed to be staring at me. I took to my heels and ran as fast as I could back to Kempi. She lay there chewing the cud, and hardly moved when, hot and excited, I flung my arms around her neck.

Shortly afterwards the children arrived, and it wasn't long before Father, Mother and Granny came in sight.

'Where is Kitto, Shanta?' Mother asked immediately.

But I hadn't seen Kitto, and he always kept close to Mother.

'He'll turn up,' said Father, 'we've been here several days and he knows the place. But you shouldn't have let go of him in the crowd.'

Granny said nothing. We sat and waited in silence.

The other people from our village came back and went to their sleeping-place. Nobody had seen Kitto. Mother began to cry behind her sari. She got up and said:

'I'm going out to look for him. Perhaps the lights bewildered him, and he is crying somewhere by himself.'

Granny got up too.

'I'll go with you,' she said, 'but Shanta must stay here and look after him if he comes back.'

I happened to look at the children. They were sitting up in the cart, wide awake. The boy had his arm round the girl. Father rose to his feet and looked as if he were going too. When the boy saw this, he stood up in the cart and said a great deal in his strange language. At last he jumped down, ran to Father and clung to his legs as if to prevent him from going. But Father pushed him away and went over to the station.

Several times in the course of the night Mother and Granny came back, and each time they were dreadfully disappointed at not finding Kitto. By dawn, Mother was almost out of her mind with weariness and sorrow. Nobody had slept, and no one thought of food.

The neighbours were packing up and harnessing their beasts to the carts. Soon they would begin the journey home. They were sorry for us, but there was nothing they could do.

'Go to the police,' they advised Father.

'They will certainly want more money than I've got,' answered Father.

'Perhaps they won't want money at all,' said Granny.

But Father was doubtful, and didn't go to the police. All day long, he sat in the station and watched the travellers, as if he expected them to have Kitto hidden in their boxes and bundles.

Mother and Granny walked and walked, searching street after street. They looked beneath flights of steps and behind rubbish heaps. They made enquiries in the bazaar and in the maharajah's park, but no one could tell them anything about Kitto.

The children stayed in the cart the whole day except when a train arrived. Then the boy jumped down and ran along behind it, and the whole time it was in the station he ran up and down beside the coaches. I followed him once to see what he was doing, and so I saw something I would otherwise never have known about. Beggar-boys and men with things to sell were squatting beside the railway lines. When a train started, they jumped on it at the last minute, and as it gathered speed, they clambered nimbly on to the roof or under the coaches, and hung on tightly. They had no tickets, and if the man in the train caught sight of them he got very angry and pushed them off. Once a train was halted and inspected above and below.

In the evening, the yogi I was afraid of came across the station square. He caught sight of Father and asked:

'You're not on the way home yet?'

'As you can see, I'm still here,' said Father, without looking up or greeting him.

'What is keeping you in the town now that the festival is over?' asked the yogi again.

'My son is lost,' answered Father in a low voice.

'Your son is lost?' The yogi didn't look at Father. 'You'll get him back. Boys like running around.'

'But my son is very young and not used to the town,' said Father.

'May the gods give you a long life and many sons,' said the yogi, as he turned and quickly went on his way. When he was half way across the square, he stopped and shouted:

'One day very soon I shall come to the village with your brother-in-law to cast the horoscope for your children.' He strode off with his coat swinging and disappeared in the crowd in the narrow street.

It was not until it had become quite dark that evening that Mother and Granny came back to our camp under the palm trees. Granny unrolled the sleeping-mat and made Mother lie down for a little while. I wondered if she were ill. Tears ran down her face and she kept moaning. Granny sat beside her and stroked her hair. I wanted to be comforted too, and crept close to Granny.

When Mother had fallen asleep, Granny's strength seemed to leave her. She sank down, hiding her face in her hands, but I had to talk to somebody so I whispered:

'Granny, do you think someone has stolen Kitto?'

Granny wept silently.

'Perhaps the gods will send him back to us, child,' she said.

Soon afterwards we were all asleep from exhaustion.

In the middle of the night, I was awakened by someone crying and pushing me. It was Kitto, dirty and with tears streaming down his face. The stranger boy was trying to wake Mother. She jumped up.

'Kitto, Kitto! The gods be thanked, if it really is you!'

She flung her arms around him, and lifted him up and dried his tears with her sari. Then she hugged him to her, and wrapped her sari round him as if to hide him.

Father and Granny and I gathered round them. It was almost unbelievable that Kitto had really come back again.

The little girl was sleeping soundly in the rice-straw, but the boy was busy getting the bullock on to its feet. It was obvious that he wanted us to leave at once. Father watched him for a moment and then said:

'That boy knows the town better than we do. Let's get away from here.'

It took only a few minutes to pack all our things and load them on to the cart. Kempi was tied to the back, and Father turned the cart in the direction of the station. But the boy wouldn't have that. With gestures and signs he showed us that we should take the other way by the side of the railway. By this means we should be in the right direction without driving through the streets of the town.

For a long time after we had come to the road that led to the village by the dam, Father was still hurrying the bullock along.

Kitto was whimpering. He had many bruises, and his legs had been bound. At first he hardly seemed to know us, but at day-break he became a little calmer.

It was only then that I realized that we were taking the children back to the village with us. Would Father really permit it? Or had the grown-ups forgotten all about them? I crept close to Granny and whispered: 'The children!'

Granny whispered back:

'I had been afraid that your father wouldn't take them with us but now it has happened quite naturally. If it hadn't been for that boy, we should never have seen Kitto again.'

'Where do you think he found him, Granny?'

'That's not easy to say. Perhaps in the house of a man he himself had run away from, for it wouldn't surprise me if he had been stolen in the same way as Kitto.'

'If Kitto was stolen, he will be able to tell us about it when he wakes up,' I said. But Granny whispered:

'We mustn't talk to Kitto about it. He must forget it. When the boy has learnt our language he will tell us many things.'

Mother was still holding Kitto fast. He whimpered in his sleep:

'Yogi bad, yogi beat Kitto, no, no, don't burn Kitto's foot.'

As the day went on, we became less anxious. Father took his sickle and cut the top off the last coconut. We shared the contents, and at one place the animals were watered at the tank. That was the only halt we made before we came to the village by the dam.

The old woman in my uncle's house had been waiting for us since the day before. When Father told the story of Kitto, everybody was very glad that it had had a happy ending. My uncle too had been in the town with the boys. After the procession he had left them there to go back to school. He had met the yogi, and decided that they should very soon go to our village to make the arrangements for the wedding.

I like to remember that evening in my uncle's house. We were one big happy family. In the women's room, we chattered and laughed as women do when the men are not there. The old woman and her daughter admired my diamond and the bracelets and the new saris, and everyone agreed with Granny when she said:

'The proper wedding ornaments are those the village silversmith makes.'

The old woman told us that at first my uncle's eldest son had been very angry that they thought of giving him a village girl as a wife. But when his father promised that Shanta should be sent to school as soon as she came to the village by the dam, he agreed. The old woman thought that it would be best for me to come to their house as soon as the arrangements for the wedding had been made. The boy wanted to see the girl before the wedding, and it would be as well to let him have his way in this. One could never tell what ideas these modern young people would get into their heads.

The next morning, when everything was ready for our homeward journey, my uncle said:

'My mother, the old woman, wishes to see the house where her daughter lives. When we come to arrange the marriage we will bring her with us.'

It made my mother and all of us very happy that the old woman wanted to visit us. Chattering and laughing, we took our leave. Everybody in my uncle's house came with us to the end of the village, and we waved as long as we could see each other. Now we were really on the way home. Our journey had lasted only two weeks, but I had experienced so much that it felt like years.

We reached the village late in the afternoon. The other families who had been to the festival had arrived two days earlier. Everyone knew about Kitto's disappearance, and they crowded round us at once to hear how he had been found again.

Kitto was delighted to be home. As soon as he got out of the cart, he ran to the other children and began to tell them about the railway and the shining rails.

The stranger children remained sitting in the cart and looked with scared eyes at all these new faces. But when Father untied Kempi and began to unyoke the bullock, they clambered down and stood hand in hand in the middle of the street. When the men saw them, they asked Father many questions.

'Do they belong to your family?' 'Why have you brought them with you?' 'What caste do they belong to?' Father gave vague answers. Perhaps he already regretted that they were here.

Granny went forward and took the stick out of the latch, and opened the door of our house. Then she called the children:

'Come in. This is our house.' Of course they didn't understand what she said, but they ran up to her at once. When they came in, she found an old sleeping-mat which she spread on the floor in front of the rice-jars. She sat down on the mat, patted it and said: 'I live here.' But they didn't understand until Mother took them both by the hand and made them sit down on it.

The whole of that first evening, they sat silently in the same place and watched what we were doing.

It was easy to see that the house had been empty for some time. The black snake's lid was dry and full of dust. A heap of leaf-plates were scattered over the hearth.

'The rats have been busy,' said Granny.

'The brutes have been in one of the rice-jars too,' said Father.

There were no rats in my uncle's house. There were many other things, too, that were different from our house, and it certainly wasn't only because they were richer. Why weren't there any rats? Perhaps there weren't any in the village?

Granny must have been thinking the same thing, for she said to Father:

'Ask your brother-in-law why there are no rats in his house. In this village there are more and more of them every year. They eat the rice in the fields and bite people while they are asleep.'

'It will be difficult to keep them away from Shanta's wedding clothes,' said Mother thoughtfully.

It was high time to go to the well if we were to get back before darkness fell.

'Carry one of the pitchers for your mother, Shanta,' said Granny. 'She mustn't work as hard as she used to.'

'Don't say that, mother-in-law,' said Mother quickly. 'The other women will gossip and say that I'm good for nothing.'

As soon as we came to the well, the women began to question us about our journey, and the festival, and my marriage. Mother told her tale and answered their questions, and before anyone realized it, it was dark. Because Mother was expecting a child, we had to be very careful not to meet any spirits on our way home.

That evening, it was difficult to get Kempi into the yard. She had grown accustomed to sleeping in the open, and struggled when Granny tried to lead her into the darkness under the roof. We all had to lend a hand in pushing and pulling before she came in to her usual place. The bullock was more docile. He went in of his own accord, lay down and at once began to chew the cud.

Father unrolled the mat on the terrace. It was too late to go and look at the field and the land by the river. The men hadn't eaten yet, so Father sat down to play with Kitto.

Granny lit the fire under the rice-pot, Mother put the rice in, and I laid out the leaf-plates. After the meal, there was lively talk on the terrace about the city dwellers and the strange life they live.

Suddenly I felt sleepy. When Granny noticed this, she said: 'There's milk in the pot.'

I went indoors and filled the black snake's lid, and after that I stroked Kempi and the bullock. Everything in the village was as it used to be. Soon I fell asleep, and dreamt that I was going to school in the village by the dam.

The following weeks were spent in working in the field and cleaning the house.

'If my mother comes to visit us, our house must be tidy,' said Mother.

'You are right, Kamala,' answered Granny, 'let us make the house look as nice as we can.'

We put fresh clay in the old holes in the floor. We cleaned the open courtyard and whitewashed the water-trough. The walls in the living-quarters were whitened too, and so were the stones of the hearth. They were black again before the rice was cooked. Mother and Granny wove two new mats of palm leaves, and I sewed so many leaf-plates that there would surely be enough for the rest of the year.

Every evening, when I went with the women to the well to fetch water, I looked down to the road that led to the river to see whether my uncle and the old woman were on their way. My mother too watched the road, but we never showed our disappointment that they didn't come.

Father was busily occupied with the new land by the river.

It could produce two rice crops a year if it got sufficient water. But the water had to be carried up from the river, and that was heavy work. We all had to help. The stranger children went with us everywhere. The boy liked to follow Father, but he always kept at a polite distance. He was smaller than I was and very slight; all the same, he carried one pitcher of water after another up to the field all day long.

For a long time Father behaved as if he didn't see him. But one day, when the sun was high, he stopped on the road to the river with the empty water-pitcher in his hand. He looked at the boy and said reflectively:

'Perhaps it would be a good idea to make a bascule-well. The boy is the right size to stand on the cross-bar.'

By the house wall at home there lay a tree-trunk of the kind that is often used as a corner post in a new house. In the evening, Father got the leopard-hunter and two other men from the village to help him to carry the post down to the river. The next day he dug a deep hole not far from the water. With everybody's help we pushed the post into the hole and set it upright. Then the earth was well trampled down round it.

Now Father went home and fetched a longer and much thinner post, which he fastened securely in such a way as to make a seesaw over the thick one. If you stood on the crossbar with one leg on either side of the supporting post, it would both move up and down and turn round. Granny fastened her water-pitcher to one end of the cross-bar; when it was pushed down, it reached over the river bank into the water.

Father looked at his work with satisfaction.

'Now all we need to do is to dig a couple of ditches at one end of the field,' he said, 'so that the water can run of its own accord where we want to use it.'

The boy watched attentively everything that was going on.

He helped where he could, and the girl followed at his heels. When the seesaw was ready, he talked excitedly to her in their own language, and the word 'picota' came over and over again in his speech.

'Picota,' said Father, 'that's the word that people up in the North use for a bascule-well.'

He pointed at the seesaw and repeated 'picota'.

The boy nodded and smiled. Then he became embarrassed because Father was talking to him. He raised his hands to his forehead and bowed low.

Suddenly he had an idea. He pointed at the cross-bar and at himself, and pretended to be standing on a seesaw. Father nodded. Agile as a monkey, the boy jumped on to the plank and placed himself on the seesaw. This was work he understood. One pitcher of water after another came rapidly up from the river. Father took the water and poured it on to the field.

At the time when the rice had to be watered, the boy stood on the picota every day. He worked so hard that the water streamed down his thin body. Father and he began to talk together in a language which was a curious mixture of known and unknown words. They always worked together now, while the girl was more and more with Mother. The village soon forgot that they had not always belonged there.

At last, one evening when Mother, the girl and I were going to the well to fetch water, we saw a cart coming along the road from the river. It was no one from our village. Mother stood in the road and waited, and I took her pitcher and went on alone.

When the cart arrived, I saw that Mother was greeting my

uncle and the yogi. The old woman was lifted down, and she and Mother embraced each other in the middle of the road. But the girl, who was standing by Mother, ran back to the village as fast as she could. My water-pitchers were heavy and made me walk slowly. As soon as the old woman caught sight of me, she came to meet me. She looked at the pitchers and touched my face, and the first thing she said was:

'I did right when I chose you as a wife for my son's eldest son.'

I put the pitchers down and greeted her respectfully. My uncle smiled kindly, but the yogi's glance made me afraid.

It was time to go home.

'If you will get into the cart, Mother, we will drive on,' said my uncle.

'Can I not walk on my own feet beside my daughter?' answered the old woman angrily. 'You drive on and greet your brother-in-law. I will follow with Kamala and Shanta.'

The men drove the oxen forward. We followed with the water-pitchers. The yogi didn't go right into the village. He sat down under a tree at the village boundary to talk to the men as they came home from the fields. The boy unyoked the oxen and led them in beside Kempi. Then he spread the mat out on the terrace, and Father and my uncle sat down to have a talk. The boy wanted to sit down too, but he was disturbed the whole time by the girl, who whimpered and clutched his loin-cloth and tried to tell him something. He only half listened to her. Perhaps she was afraid of the strangers?

Granny invited the old woman to sit beside the hearth. It was getting dark inside the house, and the fire under the rice-pot cast our shadows on the wall. I wondered what the old woman thought of our house. It was very humble compared with hers. Did she notice that the floor was clean and that there were new patterns on it? I hoped the rats would keep away that night.

98

'Sit down beside your mother, Kamala, and talk to her while I prepare the meal,' said Granny. 'Even if our house is humble she will feel the warmth of a daughter's care.'

'Your house is like the house where my children were born,' answered the old woman, 'and that was not a humble house.'

'You have lost the habit of living in the same house as the animals,' said Granny.

'It is a good custom that men and beasts should live together,' was the answer. 'The man who has no affection for his animals will fare badly in his next life.'

'But you cannot have your evening bath,' said Mother, 'it is too late to go to the tank.'

'This house is clean,' answered the old woman. 'My daughter will bring me water to wash my mouth and hands before and after the meal. What more do I need?'

Granny had set me to work to scrape the inside out of a coconut. She herself was busy making a sweet dessert that was prepared only for very special guests. We squatted on the floor as is the custom when preparing food. Round us were cooking-pots and wooden platters and carving knives.

'It is simple fare we offer you,' said Granny, 'but it is the best we have.'

'You have rice cooking over the fire, vegetables and spices have been prepared, and milk, coconut and sweetmeats are here too. Can anyone wish for more?' came the reply.

She wrapped her sari round her legs, rested her elbow on her knee and propped her chin on her hand. 'I made the right choice for my son's eldest son,' she said as if to herself. There was silence for a while; then the old woman asked after Kitto.

'Kitto is with the boys who are minding the goats in the jungle,' answered Mother.

Suddenly the boy and girl came in through the door. The girl was crying and the boy had almost to carry her. Mother wanted to take the girl in her arms, but the children passed by her and went and sat on the mat in front of the rice-jars. The girl clung tightly to the boy and wouldn't be comforted. He kept his eyes on the door as if he expected some danger to appear.

'Little girl,' called Mother, 'come here!'

'Don't go,' said the boy quickly, 'yogi here, yogi wicked.'

Granny covered her face with her sari and went to the doorway. I stole after her.

The evil-looking yogi had come. He had sat down on the mat with the men.

'I am glad the yogi has come with me to your village. It is reassuring to have a holy man to cast the children's horoscope,' said my uncle.

'It's a good thing to get the matter settled quickly,' said Father.

'There will be no lack of rupees if the papers are ready for us to read this evening,' said my uncle to the yogi.

The sun had set, and the yogi's face couldn't be clearly seen in the shadow under the lean-to. Kitto came back from the jungle. He went up on the terrace and bowed before my uncle. As he passed in front of the yogi, he stiffened. He opened his mouth to shriek, but no sound came. Then he turned round and fled through the door into the house. He knocked Granny down, jumped over the food on the floor, and ran behind the rice-jars. Only then did he begin to cry.

Father came in and said angrily: 'Kitto, where are you? Come here.'

But Kitto stayed where he was. It was the boy who spoke to Father.

'Kitto knows yogi, yogi wicked, steals children, takes them far away on the train.'

'Nonsense,' said Father, 'my brother-in-law knows this yogi.'

'Doesn't know yogi at night,' answered the boy, 'at night beats children, teaches them to steal, teaches them to beg.'

'If he had stolen Kitto he wouldn't have risked coming here,' said Father.

'In yogi's house always dark,' explained the boy, 'children don't see yogi. Other men help, steal children, bring them home. Yogi beats children in dark, speaks in dark. Yogi thinks, Kitto young, Kitto not recognize yogi, yogi not think he meet boy from North in Kitto's village.'

'The yogi will beat me, the yogi will beat me,' wept Kitto behind the jars.

Outside the house, the men of the village had begun to assemble. At first the yogi behaved as if it was nothing to do with him. 'Children can't be relied on,' he said. My uncle was silent, but he kept his eyes on the yogi.

The men heard what the boy said, and some of them began to mutter: 'Is he a yogi? What do we know about the fellow? Anybody can go about in an orange coat. Perhaps he will steal all our children tonight.'

Suddenly Mother said: 'The children were afraid of him in the town too. Why should they say bad things about him for no reason?'

I remembered that evening when he had stood in the crowd outside the maharajah's palace. I was sure the boy was right, the yogi was a child-stealer.

The muttering rose to an angry shout. The idea of a stranger forcing himself upon them and terrifying the children! Why didn't he say anything in his own defence?

'Bring the children out here,' said one of the men. 'If he is not the man they think, they will calm down at once. Let us see whether he dares show himself to the children.'

'Kitto, come out here!' shouted my uncle.

But Kitto merely crept farther in behind the jars. Father pulled him out of his hiding place and carried him on to the terrace. Kitto shrieked and struggled, and when he saw the yogi he yelled like someone possessed of an evil spirit. The yogi looked uneasy and rose to his feet. My uncle got up too. The men from the village stood close to the terrace: some of them clenched their fists and came up the steps. Then unexpectedly the stranger boy thrust his head forward into the circle while standing half hidden behind Father. He looked straight at the yogi and spoke rapidly to him in his own language. The yogi leapt at him. Father got in between them, but behind Father's back the boy shrieked:

'I know where he hides children, he steal Kitto, I steal Kitto back again. He steal us too, travel many days in train, we never find home.'

Immediately the men fell upon the scoundrel. There was shouting and waving of arms. In the confusion, he broke away from them and rushed down the village street. The men followed hard at his heels. The dogs woke up and joined in with furious barking, but it was very dark, and he fled from them towards the jungle. Nobody wanted to follow him as far as that. They came back, disappointed; only the dogs went on barking in the darkness for a long time.

It was late before the men went in to the rice-pots that evening, and as soon as the meal was over they gathered at our house again. We women hadn't finished eating when the first of them arrived.

Those men who had never been to the town were astounded that such wicked things could really happen. The boy had to tell in his halting speech how the 'yogi' had stolen them far away in the North at the foot of the mountains. How he had taken them with him in the train for many days until they came to the maharajah's city. How he had ill-treated them and forced them to steal and beg, until at last one day they saw their chance to escape. The yogi didn't watch them closely. Their home was so far away, and he knew that they would have to come back to him if they didn't want to starve.

But luckily they had met people from a village. Village folk are not so used to beggars, therefore they show more pity than people in a town. Now all the boy wanted was to be allowed to work for Father until he was old enough to go and look for his own town and his family. All he knew about it was that he must go North to the foot of the mountains.

The men didn't stay long. There was an unusual air of excitement in the village. Women and children dared not remain alone in the house. The evil stranger was somewhere out there in the darkness, and just as at harvest-time, the men stayed awake for most of the night.

When they had all gone, my uncle said:

'No one need be afraid, he will never come back to this village again.'

'Perhaps not,' answered Father, 'but he may go somewhere else and do his wicked deeds.'

'The gods undoubtedly had a reason for letting him escape from us,' said the old woman. 'Perhaps they themselves will punish him in the jungle tonight.'

'When we get home, I shall go to the police in the town,' said my uncle, 'so that they can set a watch on his house. If they don't catch him, perhaps they can catch his accomplices.'

'And free the children he has stolen,' said Mother.

'It's dreadful to think that those children have nowhere to go and will still have to beg for a living,' said Granny.

'At least they won't get any more beatings from him,' said Mother, and stroked Kitto's hair.

It was late, and we were all tired after the events of the evening. Nobody could give a thought to wedding arrangements now, but I was glad that the man with the cold eyes would have nothing to do with them. Father and my uncle were still sitting on the terrace. The old woman lay down with us on the sleeping-mat. I had forgotten the black snake, so I quietly got up again, put the milk in the lid and busied myself with the animals for a minute or two. The old woman sat up: the creaking of the new mat told me so. Perhaps she wanted to know what I was doing. Nobody said anything.

One of the children sighed in its sleep. It was comforting to lie down again close to Granny's side.

The next day was a good day. Father and my uncle compared the horoscopes. They got the teacher at the new school to help them. Everything seemed to be propitious. The final arrangements about the dowry and the wedding feast were agreed upon: the wedding was to be before the next rainy season. Mother went with Granny and the old woman to the silversmith to order a belt, bracelets and anklets of solid silver. Father was in such a good humour that he called after them:

'Let the ornaments be heavy and let the smith take pains with them.' Then he and my uncle went down to the river to see the picota and the rice.

That day I made the house finer than ever before. Because I was happy, ideas for new decorations swarmed in my fingers, and the white chalk patterns wound their way inside the house, out on the terrace, and down the steps. There was a plentiful supply of water in the pitcher, and fuel for several days beside the hearth.

The old woman praised me highly when she saw the house, and Mother was happy because she was pleased with everything. After the mid-day rest, the talk ran, as it does among women, on people and events in our village, until the old woman asked Mother a strange question.

'My daughter has doubtless taught her daughter how she must obey her husband when she is married?'

Mother was embarrassed and cast her eyes down. She did not look at her mother as she answered:

'Shanta is not very old yet.'

'But old enough to be married, so they tell me,' said the old woman, 'and just as old as you were when I gave you to your husband.'

Mother bowed her head.

'There is still time before we send her to your house,' said Granny. 'Kamala will instruct her during that time.'

The old woman appeared to be satisfied. A little later she said:

'Shanta could come to my son's house during the festival of lights. The boy celebrates it at home; it would be a good thing for the girl to be there too.'

I understood that even if the grown-ups had settled all the arrangements, the whole thing would finally depend on whether the boy liked me. I should have to pay great attention when Mother began to tell me how to please a husband. It would be very embarrassing if he didn't like me, and then I shouldn't go to school either.

'We will send Shanta to you if you wish it,' said Granny, addressing the old woman. But Mother said: 'You must send her home again a few weeks before the wedding, Mother.'

And thus the women's part of the wedding arrangements was settled.

The village children stayed indoors that day, and the men at their work were on the look-out to see whether any stranger came along the road, or over the plain. All this talk about the wedding had almost made me forget the events of the previous evening, but it was obvious that the boy remembered them. Even before it was time to go to the well, the two children came in, and while we were fetching water, Father and my uncle returned from the river.

The grown-ups sat on the terrace for a long time in the warm darkness. But my head was so full of thoughts that I soon went indoors to be alone on the sleeping-mat.

The next morning, my uncle and the old woman began their journey back to the village by the dam. We went with them as far as the end of our village, and it was agreed that our whole household should accompany me to my uncle's house in the days before the festival of lights. Nobody had any idea that everything would turn out quite differently.

In the following weeks, Mother and Granny talked about the wedding the whole time. They told me how I was to behave during the ceremony itself: I must not look at my husband, but keep my eyes fixed on the ground; I must not uncover my hair, but keep my sari over it. They told me how I should greet him when we were married by covering my face as soon as he came into the room. I must remember never to say his name. It was very important that his food should be served according to the custom of his house. Mother and Granny were so excited that I couldn't understand all their instructions.

I was taught how to weave mats although my fingers were still small and slender. I often had to prepare food quite on my own, and decide for myself whether the rice was cooked. I had to pay careful heed to the way in which Mother and Granny sacrificed morning and evening at the house-altar where we had a picture of Krishna. But first and foremost, it was impressed upon me early and late that I must listen attentively to what the old woman had to teach me, because it would be she who managed my uncle's house for many years to come.

I began to notice which of the women at the well were married and which had no husband. Before, I had only thought of them as grown-ups who didn't understand anything. Now I began to understand myself that they were very different. Some were clever, others were always angry. Some smiled, others were miserable. In some houses there were many children, in a few there were none at all. Women's lives were very different.

A woman who wore a white sari was, of course, a widow. If her hair was shaved off, and if she wore no ornaments, then one knew that she was also childless. These women usually kept to themselves and rarely spoke.

There was one woman who had been brought back to the village a short time ago by her husband. She had been married to him for five years but had had no child; therefore he grew tired of her and sent her home again. One evening when I was late in coming to the well, she was sitting on a stone with her pitcher beside her.

'Greeting, Shanta,' she said. 'You have become a big girl since I went away.'

'My mother says I am grown up now,' I answered.

'You are as old as I was when I went away from the village

with my husband,' she said, 'and now I hear that it is you who are to be married and go away. May the gods be more generous to you than they were to me.'

'Were your husband's people unkind to you ?' I asked.

'My husband's family treated me like a daughter. They had a big house and there were many servants. No one required any work of me.'

'Didn't your husband like you ?' I asked quickly.

'My husband said that I was beautiful, and he would never have anyone else to serve his food, but the gods did not let me bear a child. He was patient with me for many years, but a man must have a son to light his funeral pyre,' she concluded sadly.

'Will you ever go back to him ?' I asked.

'No, Shanta, my husband has already taken another wife.'

Suddenly she rose to her feet and quickly placed her pitcher on her head.

'Come to my mother's house tomorrow,' she said, 'and I will show you my wedding sari,' She turned and walked away to the village.

The following afternoon, I took the water-pitcher as I was accustomed to do, but I went to the woman's house before I went to the well. She was sitting outside, chopping wood. The house had no terrace, and looked poverty-stricken.

By the wall of the house sat a very old man, staring in front of him with sightless eyes. The woman got up at once and invited me to come in. Everything was very clean, but there was no decoration anywhere. Beside the fire sat an old woman, rocking herself to and fro. She had a great abscess on her leg which made her groan with pain.

'My mother has bad blood in her leg,' said the young woman. 'I have put earth and leaves on it as the neighbours said I should do, but the poison won't come out. A doctor could cut it out, I have seen it done in my husband's village, but there is no doctor here. We must wait until it comes out of its own accord, but it gives her a great deal of pain.' Sadly she stroked her mother's arm.

From a tin box at the back of the room she took out a sari. It was the colour of a lotus and as fine as the one I had seen in the town.

'My husband gave it to me as a wedding present,' she said, smoothing it carefully. Then she sat down and unfolded it in front of me. It was certainly the most beautiful sari in the village.

'I am the only one to do the work in the house and the field,' she said. 'My father is blind and my mother is old. I shall never wear this sari again.' She folded it carefully and put it back in the box.

The old woman moaned.

'Come, it is time to go to the well,' said the young woman, and she stroked her mother's face before she took up the pitcher.

I was filled with a fear I couldn't explain. When I crept close to Granny's side that night, I told her about the beautiful sari, and I think she understood what I didn't dare to say about my fear, for she said:

'The gods will be kinder to you, little girl.'

But now I was afraid in earnest, and I whispered:

'I never want to leave this house and the village, Granny.'

'My girl,' said Granny, 'no one can prevent a child from growing up. You have grown up since the last rainy season.' And I knew it was true.

One day the rumour reached us that many people were sick in the villages to the East. A week later, there came a message from my uncle's house that the infection had spread to the village by the dam. As yet no one was sick in their house, but in other houses there were many who were ill.

It began in the same way each time. The sickness caused pains in the stomach, and afterwards there came a fever which grew worse and worse until finally the victim fell into a coma. Many died.

A week later we had another message. The boys had come home from the town, but there was no festival of lights in the house. The old woman was sick, and her daughter-in-law too was unwell. The funeral pyres were already burning beside the river. There were many dead in the village.

A few days later, the sickness came to our village. The old man in the young woman's house was the first to be attacked. The new teacher said that the infection came from the water, and so only a few women went to the well. But no one could manage without water for long, and Granny said:

'If the sickness is in the water, it must also be in other things. In the air, in the rice and in Kempi's milk.' And so I still went to fetch water every evening.

Every day we heard of fresh cases, now in one house, now in another. Little work was done in the fields or in the houses. People walked about quietly, and in the evening they talked in low tones on the terraces. The constant question was:

'Why have the gods sent the sickness to us? How can we appease their wrath?' Frequent sacrifices were offered on the house-altars, and the oil-lamp in the temple was tended with care, even after the swami had fallen sick, but no one thought of any common effort such as we had made when we sacrificed for rain. Every day more and more funeral pyres were seen at the burning-place by the river. Soon it would be difficult to buy fuel, and what then?

It was more than two weeks since we had had news from my uncle's village. 'We are all in the hands of the gods,' said Granny. On that day the leopard-hunter fell ill, and in the night we heard him moaning. The following day, Father came home from the field feeling very tired. He didn't eat his rice, but went outside and vomited. Afterwards he came in and lay down on the sleeping-mat. We sat by the hearth and watched him anxiously. The children and Kitto didn't want food either, but Father said:

'Eat now, I shall be well again tomorrow. The sun was very hot in the field today, that is the only cause of my sickness.' Mother, Granny and I ate a little rice, but that was merely to reassure the children. The animals were restless too. Father moaned in his sleep now and then. The black snake didn't come that night, or ever again. Nobody spoke, but we didn't sleep either. From time to time Mother got up and gave Father a little water. About daybreak I fell asleep, and dreamt that I went to my uncle's house in my new sari with all my wedding finery. My uncle opened the door to me. His eyes were tired and sorrowful as he said:

'My mother, the old woman, is dead, and the gods have taken my eldest son also.' I awoke. Perhaps I had been weeping, for Granny stroked my head and said:

'Little girl, why are you crying?' My terror was still with me, and I crept close to Granny.

'Someone is dead in my uncle's house,' I answered.

'You have been dreaming,' she said, 'perhaps the dream isn't true.'

As the day went on, Father became worse. Fever tormented him so that he tossed to and fro on the mat, but the sweat wouldn't break out. Mother sat beside him the whole time, and moistened his lips now and then. Before evening, all three children were sick and in the course of the night Mother began to vomit. There was no doubt about it any longer, the sickness had come to our house.

Granny and I were busy doing what we could to relieve the others. We hadn't the means to give any real help to them. Only the doctor in the big city could have done that, but he was much too far away. Besides, it was not only we who needed him but the whole neighbourhood.

During those days Granny and I hardly talked to each other at all. I had a suspicion that she was ill, too, but by an effort of will she kept going so that she could help the others. The children were doing best: it seemed that they had passed the crisis. Now they lay weak and listless, staring at the ceiling. Mother was bathed in sweat, and did not recognize us. Father grew weaker and weaker.

One morning, Granny didn't get up. When I tried to speak to her, she only said: 'Cook rice for the children.'

I cooked some rice but they didn't eat it. That evening, I became ill. How many days went by I do not know. When I came to myself again, the boy was sitting by the hearth and cooking rice. Mother sat by Father's side, weeping. She looked worn and emaciated. I could not get up, but I realized at that moment that Father was dead. The next time I woke, the boy tried to give me some rice to eat. He gave some to the girl and to Kitto as well, but Mother didn't eat anything.

Slowly I began to take part in the life of the household again. The boy fetched water and cooked rice for all of us. Granny lay in a stupor, and Father was dead. It was my first experience of death in our house. I had often seen village people carry someone to the funeral pyre by the river, but this time it was my father who would never walk and speak again. Mother never moved from his side. I almost believed that she was dead too. It was not until long afterwards that I fully understood how hard it is for a woman when her husband dies. Suddenly I heard Mother crying, and then I began to cry as well because she was crying. Perhaps too it was because the thought had come to me that Granny might die like Father.

Even though I was still weak, I knew that it was I who must nurse Granny and arrange for Father's funeral pyre. Mother sat without moving and perhaps Granny would never wake again. Now I would have to show that I was grown up. The funeral pyre must be lit, so that my father's journey into the next life might be a good one. But I hardly knew what custom demanded. I had heard so often that a man must have a son to light the pyre, but Kitto knew still less about it than I did. If I asked Mother anything, she did not answer or else she lamented:

'My husband is dead. My children are fatherless.'

The smell of death was in the house. I sat and thought about whom in the village I could go to for help. Obviously there was nobody. Every house had its own dead. The boy sat and looked at me, waiting for me to say something. Suddenly it came to me that the one person who could help was my uncle. Could the boy find the long way along the river to the village by the dam? It would be four days and nights before my uncle could get here, but there was no other solution. I didn't know that long before that time the choking smell of death would completely fill the house. The boy understood at once what I wanted him to do. He got up to make arrangements for the pyre before setting out on his journey.

Just at that moment, we heard sandalled feet walking down

the village street, and then footsteps on the terrace. My uncle stood in the doorway. He looked different from usual; his eyes were tired and there were deep furrows in his face. There was no need to tell him how things were with us. He understood immediately that we needed his help.

The boy went with him into the village. It was dark when they returned. Without saying a word, they ate the rice I put before them. Before my uncle went to the sleeping-mat, he said:

'Everything has been done so that your father's funeral pyre can be lighted tomorrow at daybreak.'

Early next morning, my father's body was carried down to the river. The pyre had not been made on the burning-place, but on his own land under the palm trees beside the well. My uncle showed Kitto what a son has to do at his father's funeral pyre. Mother wept bitterly, and the stranger boy stood silently by my uncle's side. Granny was still very ill, and saw nothing.

The fire was tended for the whole day, and at evening my uncle and Kitto scattered the ashes over the river. The rice was growing abundantly in the field behind us. That field had been my father's pride. Who would harvest the rice now? As we went home along the edge of the field, my uncle said:

'The rice is ripe, it must soon be harvested.'

That evening on the terrace, my mother spoke for the first time for a long while. She sat down beside my uncle, and said:

'The gods have punished me heavily; may they grant that I keep my mother-in-law.'

'The gods have punished many,' answered my uncle quietly. 'The sickness has taken your mother and my eldest son.'

Nothing more was said, and I did not know how I should hide my sorrow. It was time to sleep, but I did not lie down on the mat. I sat with my arms around Kempi's neck, and when her munching had soothed me a little, I began to think about the future. Nobody would think now of sending me to my uncle's house to go to school. Who would cultivate the land and provide the food here? The rice is ripe, my uncle had said. Who would harvest it?

My uncle stayed with us for a few days longer. The rice was gathered and taken to the threshing-floor, and then he had to go home again to the village by the dam. Granny was up now, and was slowly beginning to get her strength back. The sickness disappeared from the village and the neighbourhood, but every house had had its funeral pyre. The days went by, even though our life had changed since Father died.

The men no longer gathered on the terrace in the evening to talk. Who was there to talk to? There was no man in the house. Every day the boy worked on the threshing-floor with the bullock and Kempi, and the rest of us helped him as best we could. The boy was used to the work in the fields, and though he was small, none the less it got done. My uncle had promised to help us when the tax for the land by the river had to be paid. Father had told him how the matter had been arranged, and as he understood about days and dates, we knew that he would come at the right time. However from the day the rice was in the house we began to expect him.

Usually I went to the well alone now. Mother said that the new baby would soon come. She walked heavily, and cried a great deal. What would become of us, a large family of women and children without a man in the house? But Granny said:

'Both good and evil are sent by the gods. It is not for us to question their ways.' She herself went to the well very seldom. The sickness had aged her, and she often sat quietly on the terrace. All the same, she followed closely everything that went on in the house.

One evening, when I was on my way to the well as usual, I

heard groans coming from the leopard-hunter's house. Someone must be ill. His wife came out quickly with her water-pitcher on her hip, and without giving herself time to greet me, she hurried on to the well. What was it she wanted to escape from? I crept up to the door and peeped in. In the middle of the courtyard sat the leopard-hunter. In front of him a fire was burning, and he was holding a piece of iron in the flames. When it was red hot, he took it out and pressed it hard against his foot. He groaned the whole time, but most loudly when the iron touched his foot. It was so dreadful to look at that I couldn't move from the spot. Later, I ran as if an evil spirit were at my heels, and I didn't stop until I had reached the well.

Most of the village women were gathered round the leopard-hunter's wife who stood there weeping. She told them that her husband had an evil thing in his stomach, and could neither eat nor sleep. This evil thing had gnawed and gnawed day and night until he had the idea of burning his foot. When he put it against the red hot iron, the pain went from his stomach to his foot and was not so sharp, but he kept groaning all the same.

The potter's wife, who was always so well informed about everything, pushed her way to the front of the crowd, and told how there had been a gnawing in her eldest son's stomach in just the same way before he died, two rainy seasons ago.

But the young woman who had been married in another village, said to the leopard-hunter's wife:

'Tell your husband that he must go to the doctor in the big city.'

The leopard-hunter's wife wept still more, and a woman whose house was always dirty, said:

'Listen to her. She thinks she knows everything because she has been away from the village.'

But the young woman went on:

'My father-in-law also had pains in his stomach. The doctor cut them out with his knife.'

The leopard-hunter's wife uttered a shriek, and the potter's wife said: 'Don't believe her, a woman who has not borne a child to her husband.'

All the same, most of the women insisted that the doctor could probably help.

'Why didn't you take your mother to the doctor when there was some evil thing in her leg?' the woman with the dirty house asked suddenly.

'It is a long way to the town. My mother is old and we have no cart,' answered the woman.

The leopard-hunter was not old, and he had both cart and oxen. The sun was low in the sky. I let my pitcher down into the water and pulled it up again. While I was setting it in position on my head, I saw a man approaching on the road from the river. Perhaps it was my uncle. I got to the road before the other women had filled their pitchers.

It was my uncle: I recognized him even at a distance by the brown cap and the black umbrella. He greeted me kindly, and I returned his greeting without raising my eyes from the ground. When he began to walk towards the village, I followed him at three paces' distance as my mother had taught me. I was careful too to cover my mouth the whole time with a corner of my sari. That would be most fitting if he were to turn round.

While we walked he talked to me. First he asked:

'How is my brother-in-law's mother? Has the sickness left her?'

'Your brother-in-law's mother is no longer sick, but great weariness has aged her in these last weeks,' I answered.

'Is my sister still weeping for her husband?'

'Your sister is grieving because her children have no father and because the new child will be born fatherless.' I was very careful with my answers, for my uncle was questioning me as one questions an adult.

'Has my brother-in-law's son grown during these last weeks?' he asked again.

'Kitto is thriving. He goes with the stranger boy to the field, and does not often hide behind his mother's sari.'

'And the stranger boy?'

'He is a great help to us. Thanks to him, the rice has been threshed and cleaned,' I answered.

It was dark when we got to the leopard-hunter's house. A feeble ray of light from the fire in the courtyard shone through the door on to the road. Several of the leopard-hunter's many dogs were on the terrace. Their whining mingled with the moaning that could still be heard inside the house. My uncle went up to the door. He stood there for a moment and looked at the wretched man. 'Why are you hurting your foot?' he asked.

'By Rama,' groaned the leopard-hunter, 'the pain in my foot makes the pain in my stomach less.'

'Stop doing yourself harm,' said my uncle. 'Is it possible that a man and a hunter can complain in this way?'

'The pain has been in my stomach so many days and nights that I cannot count them any longer,' groaned the hunter. 'There is a beast of prey in my stomach that tears and claws at me.'

'Why do you not go to the doctor in the town?' asked my uncle.

'If I were a rich man I could go to the doctor in the town,' whimpered the hunter.

'If you go to the hospital in the maharajah's city you will not have to pay,' answered my uncle.

'Do you think a doctor can see into my stomach and find out where the evil is ?' asked the hunter.

'A doctor has learnt how to track down a pain as you track a leopard to his drinking-place,' answered my uncle.

'And what does he do when he knows the place where the sickness is ?' asked the hunter again.

'He cuts it out and kills it, just as you kill the leopard before it kills you.'

The man moaned again.

'May the gods ease your pain and give you the understanding to go to the doctor as soon as it gets light,' said my uncle before he turned and left the house.

At home the rice was already cooked, and Mother had put leaf-plates ready for us. Since Father's death we all ate at the same time. Now, of course, my uncle had his food first, and it was I who had to ladle it out and bring him everything. I did as Mother and Granny had taught me, and he appeared to be satisfied.

'You would have been a good wife for my eldest son,' he said.

I brought him water to wash his hands, and afterwards he sat outside on the terrace. As soon as we had eaten, Granny and Mother went out to him. The children huddled in the corner, and I sat there too when the food had been put away and the hearth set in order for the night. My uncle asked Granny about the harvest, how many measures of rice we had had, and whether the rice was heavy. He thought there would be enough for the tax for a whole year, and that there would also be seed for the new crop.

'In that way the whole of the next harvest will be your own,' he said, 'but now we must see whether the land-owner's paper agrees with what my brother-in-law said to me.'

We waited for the tax-collector the whole of the next morning, but he didn't come until after the noonday rest. Several times in the course of the morning the children had been to the end of the village to look for him, and when at length he arrived they were very much amused by his curious clothes. He wore long trousers, as people in the town do, and they were made of stiff grey cotton. His shirt was orange, like a yogi's, and over it he had a white thing that Granny called a jacket. But strangest of all was the thing he wore on his head. It was round and stiff like a coconut, bordered with a brim that shaded his face.

'Look at that fellow,' said my uncle, 'he fancies himself, walking about in a helmet like a foreigner.' He pulled his dhoti tightly round his legs, and sat down on the mat with his back against the wall.

The tax-collector came up on to the terrace, and greeted us by taking off his helmet. My uncle greeted him, as others do, by folding his hands, but I noticed that he didn't raise them to his forehead, only to his breast. He invited the stranger to sit down, but the man didn't even take his shoes off before he seated himself. Completely at his ease, he wiped the sweat from his forehead with the back of his hand as he said:

'It's frightfully hot today.'

'We can expect rain in a few weeks,' said my uncle politely.

'Why don't I see the man of the house?' asked the tax-collector. 'It's no good for him to hide. I shall stay here until he shows himself.'

I remembered quite well that my father had been obsessed with the idea of owning land by the river, but had he really borrowed money from a man like this? Perhaps he was a money-lender, one of those who made their living by cheating the peasants. There were many stories in the village about such people.

My uncle sat in silence for a moment, then he said:

'My brother-in-law is dead, but he told me that he agreed to pay you ten measures of rice for ten years for the land by the river.'

'Ten measures!' shouted the collector, 'It was a hundred!'

'Have you the paper my brother-in-law put his thumb-mark on?' asked my uncle.

The tax-collector pulled a paper out of his pocket.

'Here, see for yourself,' he said.

We all stood in the doorway and listened to what was going on. My uncle examined the paper carefully. The tax-collector looked triumphant. My uncle slowly raised his head and looked at him.

'You have cheated my brother-in-law,' he said.

'Do you find anything wrong with the paper?' asked the tax collector slyly.

'The paper is all right,' answered my uncle, 'but you have written down a different figure from the one you said to my brother-in-law.'

'Your brother-in-law looked at the paper before he put his thumb-mark under it,' the fellow answered calmly.

'That is certainly true,' answered my uncle, 'for you knew that he couldn't read figures.'

'You will have to give me a hundred measures of rice or else I'll go to the police,' threatened the money-lender.

'You can't frighten me like that,' answered my uncle. 'I know that the police punish money-lenders when they find them. You can have the ten measures of rice that your master the land-owner has a claim to, and then you will give me that paper. Otherwise I shall go to the police, so that they can find out whether it is you or the landowner who is the money-lender.'

My uncle succeeded in frightening the man. He quickly handed over the paper, and my uncle took it and tore it into small pieces, while the money-lender swiftly disappeared down the street without thinking of the rice. When he felt safe, he turned round and shouted:

'Now that the paper has been torn up, you have no further right to the land.'

'Nobody cares about renting land from a money-lender,' answered my uncle. But the boy got up and went into the house. 'Land, palms, picota, all gone,' he said sadly.

At the moment we were ten measures of rice richer than we had thought, but if my uncle had not been there, the money-lender would easily have frightened us and perhaps he would have taken Kempi and the bullock away. That sort of thing had happened in the village before.

In the evening, as we sat on the terrace, Granny said to my uncle:

'It is hard that the gods took my son before they took me, an old woman, but we must thank them for giving us your help. All the same, it will be difficult for us to procure food now that we are only women and children in the house.'

'You know, mother, that my house is your house. The day you wish it, you can all come and live with me. My house is large and my fields are fruitful,' answered my uncle.

'We are grateful to you,' said Granny, 'but this house is my home. The field has given me and my family food in good times and bad. Here my children were born and my son died. You will understand that I must stay here until I die.'

'I understand, mother,' answered my uncle.

'But Kamala and the children,' continued Granny, 'they would have an easier life in your house.'

My mother had been sitting there as if she didn't hear what the conversation was about. She had been strangely listless ever since Father's death. Now she slowly raised her head and said: 'My brother is very kind, but his own family live in his house. I belong here where my children were born. If the day comes when we cannot fill the rice-jars, then I will send the children to your house.'

'My sister has the right to decide for herself and her children,' said my uncle, 'but Shanta is grown up. Perhaps she should be allowed to choose for herself.'

The grown-ups looked at me. I felt embarrassed and looked down at my lap. This was the first time I had been asked what my wishes were. When the marriage was arranged, no one had thought of asking me whether I wanted it, not even Granny.

My uncle's eyes were very kind as he said: 'Shanta, even though the plans for your marriage never came to anything, you will be welcome in my house, and will always be treated as the eldest daughter-in-law. You shall go to school as my son desired.'

Thoughts crowded into my mind about the easy life in the big house in the village by the dam, about school, and new saris.

'You must consider, Shanta,' said Granny, 'that you are young and the village here is very poor and old-fashioned. In your uncle's village a new way of life has begun; it is an easier life, and it will be many years before it comes to our village.'

My uncle nodded. 'Many years,' he said. 'Do you understand that, my child?'

Perhaps I didn't understand completely, but I knew that my family, who were sitting around me on the terrace now, could not manage without me. Granny was too old for the heavy toil in the field. Mother was listless and changed after her illness and Father's death, and she would soon have enough to do in looking after the new baby. The stranger boy was no stronger than I, and the day he was old enough, he would want to take the girl by the hand and go away to find his own village. And Kitto was only a child, approaching his fifth rainy season.

Nobody was looking at me now, but the silence told me that they were all waiting for my reply, so I said:

'My uncle shows me great kindness, but I would sooner stay in my mother's house.'

Nobody answered, nobody moved, and shortly afterwards I got up and went into the house. There lay Kempi, munching as usual. I fell asleep with my arms around her neck, and only awakened after the others had gone to rest on the sleeping-mat.

Next morning, while my uncle was preparing for his return journey, terrible groans were again heard coming from the leopard-hunter's house.

'It would be better if the poor fellow were to come with me to the town,' said my uncle, 'but I suppose he is afraid of the doctor's knife.'

'Perhaps he is more afraid of the anger of the gods,' said Granny. 'A doctor is a new-fangled thing.'

'A great deal of ancient superstition flourishes in your village,' said my uncle.

'The people are poor here, and we live a long way from the main roads. How can it be otherwise?' asked Granny.

'All the same, I will go and have another talk with him,' said my uncle.

Shortly afterwards he came back again.

'The leopard-hunter is coming with me to the town,' he said.

'He wants to walk on his injured foot, so that the pains in his stomach may go down to his leg.'

'It will be a long journey for the poor fellow,' said Granny. 'May the gods and the doctor relieve his pain.'

With his umbrella under his arm and his brown cap on his head, my uncle stood on the terrace and bade us farewell. He went down the steps and walked a little way towards the village street, but then he turned round again and said:

'I will come back after the rainy season, and if there is anything you want of me, send for me.'

The leopard-hunter came out of his door. He hobbled along the street beside my uncle. His wife stood by the wall of the house and watched them tearfully. A little farther on, my uncle turned round and called to her:

'You need not weep, he will be home again in two weeks and his pain will be cured.'

But the gods had decreed otherwise. Before the week was over, the leopard-hunter came back. He was tired and dusty, and dragged his leg. The pains in his stomach were worse than ever. At the well, his wife told us that he had gone with my uncle to the village by the dam, and then walked on to the big city. He found the hospital and the doctor my uncle had spoken of, but when he was sitting on the steps outside the doctor's door waiting to go in, he suddenly became afraid. The unaccustomed sounds of clattering instruments, and the doctor himself in his strange clothing, terrified him. There was only one thought in his head, to get home! He ran as best he could, half dazed with pain, night and day without stopping. He didn't feel hungry: he couldn't keep down anything he swallowed.

The potter's wife said: 'You see what happens when anyone tries to go against the will of the gods.'

Another said: 'He ought to drink milk mixed with the water

that comes from the cow. That will cleanse his inside.' And many other pieces of good advice were given. But the woman who had once left the village said: 'He should not have run away from the doctor's door.'

That night, while everyone in the village was asleep, the leopard-hunter hanged himself in a corner of his house. Pain had driven him out of his mind. Two bold men saw to the making of his funeral pyre, but for a long time afterwards people avoided his house, and no one would go near it after dark.

The leopard-hunter had had many dogs which he had used as bait for leopards.

'Our fathers believed that dogs carry homeless souls,' said Granny, 'and we must expect that his soul will be homeless for a long time.' So people avoided his dogs too.

Peace returned to the village after these events. The days became warmer. There was not much to do in the field, but as soon as the boy saw an opportunity, he helped elsewhere in the village. Now and then he was paid for looking after the goats in the jungle, or for clearing stones from a field. What he earned he gave at once to Granny.

'You put away, we buy land by the river,' he said.

Granny put the money away so that he could have it back when he wanted to go home to his own village. One evening he said:

'My father big rice-grower far in North, not remember name of village, work land for Kitto until Kitto grown man, then go North.'

'When you go North you will have your money,' said Granny.

'No, no,' said the boy, 'buy land by river for Kitto.'

It was a good thing for all of us that we had such a plentiful supply of rice in the jars, for we could eat our fill every day. The only one who was not well was Mother. She rarely ate the good food that Granny set before her, and most of the time she sat silent and listless by the wall of the house.

'When the child comes, she will be different,' was Granny's opinion.

The morning that Mother fell ill, Granny and I helped her into the little room at the end of the terrace where births take place. The boy was sent out to fetch the women who always help on these occasions. Mother lay groaning on an old mat inside the dark little room. The women could not really do anything for her. When at last the child was born there was not much life in it, and shortly afterwards it died.

Mother had a fever and did not know us. By the evening of the next day she was dead. I didn't touch her, but I wept. I knew now what death was, and I wept for a long time. Granny sat with Mother's head in her lap and wept too. We both remembered so many good and happy things about Mother. Kitto came in through the door. He was frightened because Mother lay there so still and strange, and he began to cry as well.

Suddenly Granny sat up and dried her eyes with her sari.

'It was surely the will of the gods,' she said.

The thought came to me that if Mother had been in my uncle's house they would certainly have sent for the doctor, but I didn't say this to Granny. Perhaps the doctor wouldn't have been able to help either.

'The sickness and my son's death took all will to live from her, and the fever did the rest, but she was a good daughter-in-law to me,' said Granny.

There was no time to sit and grieve; we had to busy ourselves with all that needed to be done. This time, however, I knew

127

what custom demanded. The boy was sent off to take the sad message to my uncle, and Granny and I went into the village to get wood for the funeral pyre. Rain could be expected any day, and in many homes the rice-jars were empty, so we managed to buy wood in exchange for rice, rice from the land by the river. Of course the men did not much care for dealing with women.

'Is there no man in your family who can help you?' they asked. But when we told them that it would be four days before my uncle could arrive, they helped us. The pyre was built well and solidly. Granny and I dressed Mother in her finest sari and laid her on a new mat of palm leaves: the palm tree had always been her pride. We strewed on it all the flowers we could find at that dry season, and in the morning the men came and carried her to the burning-place. Kitto lit the pyre, and when every-thing had turned to ashes we scattered them in the river. My mother's soul would have a good journey.

At sunset the following day, my uncle arrived. He had travelled fast, for he wanted to help us. I felt great affection for him when I saw how tired and dusty he was; all the same I was glad that we had managed everything ourselves. Granny cooked rice, but we did not eat much. Afterwards we sat on the terrace in the warm darkness. Fireflies danced in the shadows along the village street. Men smoked and chatted outside the other houses. They talked about the great sickness and whom it had taken; about the rain which would soon come; about the planting of the rice and the new harvest.

When the rains came again to the village, the girl Shanta and her family sowed their rice as they had done the year before.